AN UNEXPECTED LOVE

Kieran O'Neill, a Nashville song-writer, is in Cornwall, sorting through his late Great-Uncle Peter's house. Since being betrayed by Helen, his former girlfriend and cowriter, falling in love has been the last thing on his mind . . . Sandi Thomas, a struggling single mother, has put aside her own artistic dreams — and any chance of a personal life — to concentrate on raising her son, Pip. But as feelings begin to grow between Kieran and Sandi, might they finally become the family they've both been searching for?

Books by Angela Britnell
in the Linford Romance Library:

HUSHED WORDS
FLAMES THAT MELT
SICILIAN ESCAPE
CALIFORNIA DREAMING
A SMOKY MOUNTAIN CHRISTMAS
ENDLESS LOVE
HOME AT LAST

ANGELA BRITNELL

AN UNEXPECTED LOVE

Complete and Unabridged

LINFORD
Leicester

First published in Great Britain in 2015

First Linford Edition
published 2017

A catalogue record for this book is available
from the British Library.

ISBN 978–1–4448–3182–5

Published by
F. A. Thorpe (Publishing)
Anstey, Leicestershire

Set by Words & Graphics Ltd.
Anstey, Leicestershire
Printed and bound in Great Britain by
T. J. International Ltd., Padstow, Cornwall

This book is printed on acid-free paper

1

Kieran pushed away the remains of his weak, milky coffee, and knew if he stayed in Cornwall for very long, he'd have to get used to drinking tea. He ought to leave the Copper Kettle café right now and tidy up his great-uncle's house, but couldn't work up the enthusiasm. The prospective new housekeeper he was interviewing in the morning would have to take him as he was — or not. But if he didn't employ *someone*, his mother would be on the next flight across the Atlantic to make sure he and the house weren't falling apart.

'Do your friends tease you and call you Ginger? Mine do.'

Kieran glanced up and stared at a small red-haired boy bouncing on his heels and grinning.

'My mummy says it's rude, and they're just jealous because they're not special like us.'

Kieran suppressed an unexpected urge to laugh.

'Philip Michael, what have I told you about not talking to strangers?' A pretty young woman grabbed at the boy's hand to tug him away. Kieran's eye was instantly drawn to her. Apart from her flashing blue eyes, everything else was ruthlessly controlled — from the long black hair drawn away from her face in a tight plait, to her crisp white blouse and slim-cut dark trousers. 'I'm sorry Pip bothered you.'

'No problem.'

'We'll leave you in peace.' Her crisp tone made it clear she didn't intend to prolong the conversation. She hurried the boy away, and when Pip glanced back over his shoulder and tried to say something, the woman's voice rose sharply to silence him.

Something on the floor caught Kieran's eye, and he bent down to pick up a red yo-yo.

'Are you ready to pay, sir?'

He pulled his attention back to the waitress standing in front of him. 'Yeah, sure.' He held out the yo-yo and explained who he thought it belonged to.

'That's our Pip. He's a scatterbrain, but smart, if that makes any sense.' She shoved the toy in her apron pocket. 'His mother will be in tomorrow afternoon for her next shift. I'll give it to her then.'

Too many questions popped into his head, but he refused to care about the answers. Without another word, he thrust a handful of money at the woman and left.

* * *

Sandi ignored Pip's pleas for her to slow down, and only let up her punishing pace when they were well out of sight of the café. 'How about some nice fish fingers for our tea?'

'Again? We had them last night,' Pip moaned, 'and the night before.'

Sandi bit her tongue. It wasn't her son's fault money was tight. 'I know we did, sweetheart, but we'll finish the box tonight and I'll find something different

3

tomorrow.' The week's pay she'd just picked up at the café wouldn't cover all the bills, even with her usual juggling act. If she didn't get the new part-time job she was interviewing for tomorrow, her parents would have to bail them out again. 'All right?'

'I suppose so.'

Sandi didn't press him; sometimes things were best left alone.

'Mummy, I asked the man a question, but you interrupted.'

'That's because he's a stranger and you weren't supposed to talk to him.' Sandi crouched down level with Pip's face. 'We've spoken about this before.' At six, he was a bright, inquisitive boy — sometimes too much so for his own good. She loved his open, exuberant spirit, and it was hard to teach him caution without crushing that special side of her precious son. 'Come on.' Sandi took hold of his hand and they kept on walking. 'What did you ask him, anyway?'

'If his friends called him Ginger and teased him about his hair.'

4

Sandi stopped dead in the middle of the pavement. 'You said what? Please tell me you're joking with Mummy.' He shook his head and big tears welled up in his soft brown eyes. The best she could hope for was that the man was a tourist and they'd never see him again.

'I didn't mean ... ' A tear rolled down his cheek and Sandi felt awful.

'We'll talk about this when we get home.' Sandi hugged him and was relieved when he smiled back. Sometimes his trust in her was overwhelming, and she lived in fear of not being able to live up to it.

'Can we have a pyjama day tomorrow? Please.'

'But tomorrow's Wednesday; it's school.' She almost promised to do it on Saturday instead before remembering she'd be working in the café, and Pip would be staying with her parents again.

'Silly, Mummy, it's a teacher-training day. We get to play.'

Sandi's brain raced. At ten o'clock tomorrow morning, the vicar's wife had arranged an interview for her for the job of part-time housekeeper to Mr. O'Neill at *Gwel an Mor*, the aptly named Sea View House overlooking the harbour. Her father would be working, her mother played bridge every Wednesday, and her best friend Elly was sick — meaning she was out of babysitting help.

'Pip. Listen to me.' She'd have to turn this into an exciting game. It was time to get creative.

2

'Remember, Pip, not a word.' Sandi reiterated the plan. 'You're supposed to have a sore throat.'

'But, Mummy ... '

'But nothing.' She put a firm end to the back-and-forth conversation they'd been having since yesterday. It'd taken all her powers of persuasion, plus the promise of a chocolate bar every day for a week, to convince Pip to agree. For his part of the deal, he'd agreed to be silent and sit quietly while she spoke to Mr. O'Neill.

'Here we are.' Sandi gazed up at the imposing old house and briefly had second thoughts. Pulling back her shoulders, she lifted the heavy brass ring and knocked twice. Heavy footsteps sounded and the door opened.

'Well, hi there.'

Sandi gaped in shock. 'Oh! It's you!'

Yesterday's red-haired nemesis grinned back at her.

'Hi, young Pip. Did you get your yo-yo back? I found it after you left.'

Pip shook his head frantically and gazed at her with wide eyes.

'Is something wrong?' he asked.

Sandi couldn't back down now. 'He's got a sore throat.' She nervously smoothed down her linen skirt. 'I'm sorry I had to bring him, but … '

'No problem.' He cut off her attempt to explain. 'Kieran O'Neill. We never did get around to the formalities yesterday.' Sticking out his hand, she was forced to shake it and introduce herself in return. There was nothing weak or insubstantial about his grip — or about the rest of him, if she was honest. He wasn't a traditionally handsome man, but Kieran's bright green eyes and unkempt, floppy red hair gave him a raffish, almost piratical, look.

Remembering their first meeting made Sandi cringe. Should she bring up Pip's embarrassing question or ignore it?

'Are you going to invite us in?'

* * *

'Of course.' Kieran's mental picture of a motherly, older woman, who'd tidy up after him and cook plain, nourishing meals, flew out of the window. Sandi was as lovely as he remembered, but the glimpse of vulnerable woman underneath the brisk, competent shell aroused his interest even more. 'It's a bit of a mess, I'm afraid.' He stepped back to let them come in.

'Presumably that's why you require a housekeeper?'

There were a million ways he could answer Sandi's question, but Kieran contented himself with a brief nod.

'In the message I got from Mrs. Yardley, you weren't specific about hours and rates. We need to discuss that before we go any further.'

Kieran suppressed a smile and wondered who was interviewing whom. 'Sure. Let's go in here.' He led the way into the sitting room at the front of the house which was relatively tidy. 'How about I fix us some tea or coffee? Would you like a coke, Pip?'

The boy threw his mother a beseeching look which she squashed with a brief shake of her head.

'No, thank you. We don't need anything.' Sandi breezed past him and settled herself on the ancient red leather sofa, after first folding up a pile of newspapers and stacking them on the coffee table. Without a sound, Pip sat next to her and idly swung his legs back and forth.

'Would three hours every weekday morning suit you?'

You tell me. That seems to be the way this is going.

'I could do the necessary housework and prepare a hot meal for your lunch.'

'Sure. Sounds good to me. I'm not much for domesticity.'

Her shrewd gaze swept around the room and landed back on him. Kieran felt her examine his unironed trousers, before commenting: 'I can tell.'

'What's the going rate for domestic paragons?'

Two bright red circles of heat coloured her cheeks. Ms. Sandi Thomas wasn't used to being teased — which only made him want to do it again.

'I wouldn't know, but I charge a very reasonable ten pounds an hour.' Her chin tilted in the air. 'Pip's school starts at nine and it's about a ten minute walk so I can be here by quarter past.'

'Suits me fine. We have a deal.' Kieran noticed Pip's hand creep towards the King Arthur book he'd been reading when they arrived.

'Philip Michael.' The low words were barely audible but it was enough and the boy's small hand returned to his lap.

'Are you interested in King Arthur, Pip? Maybe when your throat's better and you can talk again we'll look at the book together.'

'I can talk now.' The words burst out. 'I don't want to play the game anymore, Mummy.' A big fat tear rolled down Pip's cheek.

The old cuckoo clock broke the awkward silence as the bird popped out to begin its eleven o'clock announcement.

'We must be going now. I've got to be at work in the café at half-past twelve, and we need to eat our lunch first.' Her blunt statement dared him to ask for an explanation.

★ ★ ★

'I'm a single mother, Mr. O'Neill, and money is tight. I really need this job. When I found out Pip's school was closed for teacher training today, I couldn't risk messing up this interview.' Sandi swallowed hard. 'There was no one to look after him, so I invented a little game to get Pip to be quiet while we talked.' The compassion written all over Kieran's face irked Sandi. She didn't want or need his sympathy. 'If you'd prefer to withdraw your job offer, I'll understand. You may not want someone in your home who isn't completely honest.'

Kieran's sudden outburst of warm, infectious laughter took her by surprise.

'I'm not perfect either, so we should suit each other down to the ground.' A broad smile creased his lean face. 'You're resourceful and determined.' His green eyes sparkled. 'I like that in a person.'

Sandi decided it was best to leave while she was ahead. Jumping up from the sofa, she grabbed Pip's hand and prepared to leave. 'I'll be here in the morning.'

'Good.' A touch of amusement laced his beguiling American accent. 'We redheads have to stick together, kid.' He ruffled Pip's hair. 'You get your mom to bring you anytime. All right?'

Pip beamed, and Sandi knew she was in trouble.

3

Kieran decided decent plumbing must've been low on his great-uncle's list of priorities as he dried off after yet another tepid bath, taken half-standing because the tub was too small. But books had obviously been at the very top of Peter's list. They overflowed from the bookcases onto every available surface, filling cupboards and teetering on chairs. His mother's orders were to sell the valuable ones and get rid of the rest so she could turn *Gwel an Mor* into a vacation home. She'd hoped having something positive to do would stop him from brooding.

He couldn't imagine what she thought he'd be brooding about — apart from the fact he was still recovering from having his hard-earned songwriting reputation and his heart simultaneously broken. He'd been a fool where Helen Ross was concerned, and she'd played him like the mandolin which had brought her international acclaim.

Kieran had moved to Nashville from West Virginia the day after he graduated high school, with one small suitcase, his guitar, and the grand sum of two hundred dollars. In between stints as a waiter and supermarket shelf filler, he'd honed his songwriting skills and changed tack like many budding singers before him. After one lucky break, he began selling occasional songs to other artists, always infusing his music with the Irish rooted bluegrass traditions he'd grown up with. He should've stuck with writing on his own, but collaboration was the name of the game these days. That was when Helen came into his life ...

Get her out of your mind. It's in the past now.

He examined the faded blue t-shirt he'd been about to put on and tossed it aside. Rummaging in the drawer he found a green one that was slightly less ancient and pulled it on over his head. His jeans were more holes than denim but he abandoned the idea of changing them too. He wasn't trying to impress Sandi Thomas.

Two loud, sharp taps rang out, and Kieran smiled to himself. Even her knock was precise and no-nonsense. He took the stairs two at a time and hurried to open the door.

'Welcome. Come on in. How about a quick cup of coffee before I give you the guided tour?'

'No, thank you.' Sandi stepped inside. 'I'm here to work.'

He'd got used to conducting business in Nashville where hospitality, good manners and friendly conversation were the cornerstones of even the most high-profile deals. 'Fair enough—' Kieran almost added the word 'honey' in the typical Southern way, but stopped himself in time. 'I don't expect you to perform miracles.' For a second he thought he detected the faintest hint of a smile. 'I never met him, but I'm guessing my Great-Uncle Peter was ... I'll call him eccentric. Books were his thing, and

I'm guessing you'll have to dust around them for now until I make a start on sorting them.'

'Why don't you show me the rooms you're actually living in, and I'll make a start there?' Her brisk enquiry stopped the idle question running through his head about whether she was one of the few people in the world who ironed their jeans. Everything about Sandi was immaculate, and he was pretty sure she'd look the same when she left after three hours' hard work. 'Do you mind if I put this in the kitchen first?' She held out a wicker basket. 'You didn't mention any food allergies or preferences.'

'As long as it's not liver or sauerkraut, I'll eat anything you put in front of me.'

'That's what I like to hear.' There it was again. A quirk at the corners of her mouth nudging towards amusement. He'd love to see her really smile. *Dangerous territory. Don't go there.* 'The kitchen?'

Kieran strode off down the long hallway towards the back of the house.

He'd get this done as quickly as possible and leave her to get on with it.

* * *

Sandi wished she didn't need this job. Her single-minded focus in life was on being the best possible mother to Pip. Nothing else mattered. But Kieran's friendly manners and intriguing Southern drawl, so smooth and low she could listen to him for hours, interested her more than they should. She didn't need him shaking her intention not to date again until Pip was grown up.

She and Mike had been far too young when they married after a whirlwind courtship and Pip's birth only weeks before their first anniversary had strained their relationship to its breaking point. Loneliness, she could cope with. But she couldn't handle a broken-hearted little boy if he got attached to a possible father-figure and things didn't work out.

'I'm afraid this is it.'

Sandi stifled a groan. Retro styles from the fifties might be experiencing a revival, but these fixtures were original in the worn-out sense. Her feet stuck to the grubby, cracked linoleum when she crossed the room to check out the ancient cooker.

'My mother's going to want a fancy new kitchen, I'm sure, but you'll have to make do with this for now.'

'It's not a problem.' Sandi took out the pork chops she'd brought and popped them into the small fridge, noticing — but not commenting on — the fact that all she saw in there were cans of soda and the remains of a takeaway pizza. 'Right. A quick tour, please. After that, I'll get your lunch in to cook before I start cleaning.'

He ran his hand over the faded pale green counter and frowned. 'This place must've seen quite a bit of life in its time. Makes you think, doesn't it?'

'Mr. O' Neill.' She pointedly looked at her watch. 'I don't mean to be rude but I have a lot to do. Could we please get on?'

For a few lingering seconds his bright green eyes rested on her and Sandi held her breath until he turned and walked away.

'The only upstairs rooms you need to bother with are the bedroom and bathroom I'm using.'

Sandi admired the graceful carved mahogany staircase as they walked up to the first floor. In its heyday, this must have been a beautiful house and only needed some tender loving care to flourish again. 'How many more are there?'

'Four bedrooms and two more bathrooms. All out of the dark ages but functional. There're also a couple of maids' rooms in the attic.'

'That would've been my place.' Sandi scoffed. 'Your rooms?'

Without a word, he opened a door to reveal a large bathroom that had obviously been converted from a bedroom at some point. She smiled behind his back as he hastily swept up a wet towel from the floor and draped it over a chair. An old claw-footed bathtub dominated the room, and she couldn't avoid Kieran's laughing eyes.

'Yep, it's too small.' He gestured at the door. 'Shall we?'

'Of course.'

'I chose the room at the end. Couldn't resist the view.' Kieran strolled down the narrow corridor. 'Tell me you wouldn't have done the same.'

Sandi recognised she was being skilfully distracted from her purpose, but his enthusiasm was infectious. Despite growing up in Cornwall, she'd never become immune to the beautiful scenery, even making good attempts at painting her own interpretations in the days when she'd had the time and the freedom to dream. She stood next to Kieran at the large bay window and blinked away tears at the sight of Penarth Bay spread out in front of them. The glittering azure sea was framed by the tiny harbour and soaring granite cliffs on either side and watched over by the small village.

'Are you okay?' Kieran's compassion moved her, and she managed to nod.

'I'm soft- hearted too when it comes to beauty — whether it's in nature, art, or music.' He turned away. 'Right. Enough time-wasting or you'll reprimand me again.'

Nothing was further from her mind, but he'd thankfully brought them back to reality.

4

Sandi blanched at the mess in the downstairs living room, and hoped Kieran meant what he said about not expecting a miracle.

'I've taken Peter's old study for my work space.' He gestured towards a door across the hall. 'You don't need to go in there.'

'But won't it get dirty?'

Kieran's expression turned serious. 'I'll deal with it myself. Thank you. I'll leave you to get on now.'

Sandi left him and returned to the kitchen. She'd had a suspicion decent cooking equipment might be sparse on the ground, and brought her own sharp knife, a chopping board and a casserole dish. Soon she had a pork casserole put together, loaded with leek, apple, carrots, and fresh herbs from her garden, topped with thick slices of potato. Sandi crossed her fingers that the oven temperature was reliable and gathered up all the cleaning equipment she could find. For the next two hours she didn't waste a moment, and at least by the end the kitchen no longer resembled a health hazard.

'Smells good. I'm starved.'

Sandi nearly dropped the hot pan of green beans she was in the middle of draining. 'Don't do that again!'

'What?'

'Sneak up on me.'

He grinned. 'Maybe I could wear a bell around my neck and ring it to announce my arrival?'

'You do talk nonsense sometimes,' Sandi blurted out, before rushing to apologise; but Kieran's full-on hearty laughter filled the room.

'Don't fret. There's nothing wrong with having a bit of fun.'

'Maybe.' Before he could continue making her enjoy herself more than she should, Sandi asked if he wanted her to serve his lunch before she left.

'Is there enough for two?'

'Yes. I made plenty, so you can eat the leftovers for supper if you want.'

'Stay and eat with me.'

'Me? With you?'

Kieran lounged against the door frame and grinned. 'I promise I have good table manners.'

'I'm sure.' Sandi heard the stiffness in her voice. 'I've got to be at the café by half-past twelve for my afternoon shift.'

'You still have to eat lunch,' he persisted.

'I don't *have* to do anything, Mr. O'Neill.' She wasn't about to share her plan to grab a yogurt on the way there: the standard lunch of busy mothers.

'Okay, I surrender. Sorry for pestering.'

Sandi hated feeling in the wrong, but wasn't about to get dragged into any further conversation today. 'Goodbye. I hope you enjoy your lunch.'

*   *   *

Kieran could have kicked himself. From the moment Sandi had arrived on his

25

doorstep this morning, swinging her basket of tricks and gleaming with purpose, he'd wanted to find out more about the woman buried underneath the cool efficient exterior. But he'd gone about it the wrong way, and wished he could hit the rewind button and start over again.

Kieran took the casserole out of the oven and set it on the counter. He'd lost his appetite now. Grabbing a can of soda from the fridge to drink, he considered his options. Sort through his Great-Uncle Peter's books. Go for a run. Tackle the garden ... None of those appealed. What he really wanted was to write down the songs burning in his brain, but he was determined not to give in. He'd better find something constructive to do today or he'd go crazy. A brainwave suddenly struck him. Earlier, he'd seen Sandi give the ancient vacuum cleaner a disgusted kick before pushing it back into the hall cupboard, so he'd go out now and buy her a new one.

Is that how you're going to win her over? It'd take a lot more than a souped-up Hoover to convince Sandi Thomas he was more than an overly-friendly American who didn't know when to leave well alone.

★ ★ ★

Sandi knew before she lifted her head from the napkins she was folding that Kieran had walked into the café.

'My turn,' Mel declared, straightening her frilly white apron and fluffing up her dyed blond hair. 'Agnes served your handsome American yesterday. I get a chance to say hello now.' She picked up her order pad and bustled away.

'She's welcome, as far as I'm concerned,' Sandi protested. 'I've got enough on my plate.'

Agnes chuckled. 'So have I, but he *is* handsome.' She nudged Sandi. 'Admit it.'

She wasn't about to admit anything.

'One cream tea.' Mel tossed off the order and sighed in Sandi's direction. 'He asked to see you.'

'Me?'

'Yes, you,' she snapped.

'I'm sure it's something to do with his house.' Mel looked slightly mollified. 'Do you want me to take the tray over?'

'No thanks. I'll bring it myself in a minute when the tea's ready.'

Sandi finished folding the napkin and set it down in the wicker basket. Her hair was tidy, but she found her fingers straying to check for any stray ends before correcting herself. As she reached his table, Kieran stood up.

'Come with me.'

'Why?'

'Please. I've got something to show you in my car. I'm parked right outside. It won't take long.'

She wanted to tell him that one of them had work to do, but his warm, honeyed drawl worked its magic and she couldn't turn him down. 'Fine. I'll need to be quick.'

Out on the street, Kieran unlocked the gleaming black car and popped open the boot. Leaning in, he pulled out a large box before setting it down on the ground. 'The man assured me this was the top model.'

Sandi read the description on the outside and laughed. She couldn't help it. She'd been won over with flowers and wine before — but never with a vacuum cleaner.

'Bingo.' He grinned. 'I knew I was right.'

She was afraid to ask what he was talking about.

'You've got the prettiest smile I've ever seen.' He fixed his sparkling gaze on her face, making Sandi blush.

'Your tea's ready, Mr. O'Neill,' Mel called from the doorway.

Kieran thanked Mel and then returned the box to its hiding place. 'I'll look forward to seeing it, and you, in action tomorrow.' He winked and breezed past her to go back inside.

For a minute, Sandi stayed rooted to the spot. If she didn't need the money, she'd run as far from Kieran O'Neill as she could right now.

5

Thank goodness it was nearly five o'clock and time to finish work for the day! Immediately, Sandi reprimanded herself. Her real job started now. She hoped Pip's day at school hadn't been too bad, so their evening would be easier.

Nursery school hadn't been too difficult for him, but ever since Pip had started proper school last year, he'd never quite fitted in. Sandi knew only too well how he felt. She'd been the same kind of serious, inquisitive child who found it hard to navigate the perils of everyday life. Trying to do her best for him, she'd invited several of his classmates over for playdates, but they hadn't been a success. They'd laughed at Pip's idea to play 'King Arthur and the Knights of the Round Table', or to wait until it got dark and identify stars through the telescope she'd got him for Christmas.

Sandi had only come into her own when she discovered the joy of art in senior school, and hoped more than anything that Pip would find his own passion one day. She'd been the first in her family to go to university, and had soaked up every class with unbridled enthusiasm. But when she met Mike at a party the end of her second year, all her plans flew out of the window, and finishing her art degree became the last thing on her mind. She couldn't allow herself to regret anything, though — because she had Pip, and her son was the best thing that ever happened to her.

She headed out of the café, grateful because it was a lovely warm day for early May, and she didn't need to bother with a coat. It was tempting to dawdle and enjoy the walk but Pip would be anxiously watching out of her parents' window for her to arrive. At least she didn't have to worry about what to cook for their tea tonight, because it was Tuesday — pasty day in the Thomas household. She and Pip had lived with her parents for the first few difficult months, but as soon she could scrape together enough money, they'd moved into their own small flat. She'd needed to cling on to some measure of independence for her own sanity, and to show Pip the importance of being self-reliant.

Her thinking led her down to the harbour, despite the fact Polkirt Street was in the opposite direction. Surely five minutes of selfishness wasn't too much to ask for out of a whole day? Sandi leaned on the wall and gazed out over the sparkling silver-blue sea, musing on how hard it'd be to capture on canvas.

'We sure don't have anything this pretty in Nashville.' Kieran's warm voice next to her shoulder made Sandi jump.

'Will you please stop doing that!'

'Sorry.' Apologetic was the last thing he sounded. 'You ever been to the States?'

Sandi shook her head. 'Hardly.'

'Sorry, I didn't mean to be thoughtless.'

'You weren't.' She wanted to kick herself. 'It's my fault. I'm too sensitive.' He'd saved her from having to beg her parents for money to get through the month. Plus, he wasn't a taxing employer, and allowed her to work as she wanted with no interference. *And he bought you a new Hoover.* 'Sometimes I don't know what comes over me.'

*   *   *

Kieran longed to rub away the worried crease between her brows, but knew better than to think he could wave a magic wand and make Sandi's life easier.

'I think we got off on the wrong foot, sweetheart.' The endearment slipped out and he could've bitten off his tongue. 'That's simply a Southern expression, similar to the way y'all use the words 'dear' or 'love' when you're being friendly.'

Sandi exhaled a heavy sigh. 'I know. And please don't keep apologising.'

Kieran briefly considered asking her if she'd join him for coffee, but noticed her glance at her watch. 'Time you were going?' For a few precious seconds he held her gaze, and thought he saw a hint of regret lurking in her deep blue eyes.

'Yes. Pip will be waiting.' A tiny flash of softness relaxed her serious features. 'And so will my pasty. My Mum always makes them on Tuesdays.'

'Your folks live here too?'

Sandi nodded. 'There've been Thomases here for generations. All the way back to the 1700s.'

'That fascinates me. The continuity. The O'Neills came over from Ireland to West Virginia back in the day to work the coal mines.' He started to talk about his family, and Sandi told him about her fishermen relatives who'd worked the waters off Cornwall before it got too hard to make a living. The conversation flowed easily between them, and Kieran didn't want it to end.

'Goodness. Listen to me rambling on.'

I am, and I love it. You're quite different when you're not thinking about being a responsible mother or employee.

'I must go. I'll see you in the morning.'

As Sandi hurried away Kieran spotted a black plastic rubbish bag on the edge

34

of the pavement but he couldn't yell out a warning in time before she tripped and fell down on her knees.

'Are you all right?' He hurried over to crouch down beside her, inappropriately amused to hear some pithy words tumbling out of his housekeeper's usually prim mouth. 'Dumb question. Sorry.' Kieran ignored her attempt to push him away and gently lifted her back on her feet.

'You can let go of me now.'

He ignored her request. 'Are you hurt?'

'My pride more than anything else.' Sandi visibly winced as she glanced down over herself. Smudges of dirt and a large rip in the right knee had ruined her black trousers.

Kieran slowly turned over her hands. 'Ouch. That looks nasty.' They'd taken the brunt of her fall and were cut and bleeding.

'Don't fuss.' She pulled away. 'Thank you for your help.'

'Let me see you home.'

Sandi snorted. 'There's absolutely no

need. It's only a few scratches.'

This was a woman who'd probably insist that childbirth merely 'hurt a little'. Kieran didn't dare to object; but, as she stepped away, Sandi stumbled. He quickly grasped hold of her. 'Right. No more arguments. I'm taking you home whether you like it or not. I've been into Truro to pick up a few things, and my car is parked around the corner.'

'Fine.' Her grudging acceptance made him smile. Sandi Thomas took stubbornness at accepting help to a whole new level.

Kieran kept his arm around her waist as they made their way slowly across the road to reach his car. 'Are you gonna tell me where to go — direction-wise, that is — or do I have to guess?' he asked as she gingerly climbed into the passenger seat.

'Up the hill. First left into Polkirt Street. Number fifty-seven on the right,' she mumbled and dabbed at her knee with a tissue.

'Yes, ma'am.' Kieran pulled away from the kerb and didn't say another word until they reached the house. He caught sight of a hand frantically waving out of the window at them. 'Someone's watching for you.'

Sandi frowned. 'Pip will be upset when he sees this.' She pointed to her knee. 'He worries about me a lot. I suppose because it's just us.' Sighing, she opened the door and picked up her handbag. 'Thanks. This was kind of you.'

He hopped out and ran around the car. 'I'm taking you to the door. Don't argue again.' The tiniest of smiles pulled at her mouth, and before he could help her, she got out and limped towards the gate.

The front door opened and an older woman stepped out onto the step. 'There you are. We'd about given up on you.' She slapped a hand to her mouth. 'Oh my goodness, what on earth have you done, love?'

'I'm all right. Don't *you* start. I took a bit of a tumble, that's all,' Sandi protested. Surprisingly, she didn't push away the hand Kieran kept on her arm, and he guessed she was more shaken up than she'd care to admit.

'Mummy! Mummy! You're late.' A fireball of excited boy pushed his way out and barrelled towards them. Kieran thrust out a hand to stop him crashing into Sandi.

'Take it easy, partner.' He hurried to defuse Pip's panicked expression when he spotted Sandi's injury. 'Your mom needs your help. How about you run along inside and find something to put on her poorly knee?'

Pip's little face lit up. 'Nana has plasters with dinosaurs on 'specially for me. They make everything better.' He disappeared back indoors and Sandi threw Kieran a grateful smile.

'Are you going to introduce your knight in shining armour?' Mrs. Thomas's archly phrased question reminded him sharply of her daughter.

'Kieran O'Neill.' He stuck out his hand. 'I'm Peter Trudgeon's great-nephew. Sandi's helping me out at the house.' He grinned. 'Rescuing damsels in distress is my stock-in-trade.'

Mrs. Thomas cracked a smile and he wanted to punch his fist in the air. Maybe winning over her mother would help him get to Sandi. *What for? You're only here until the fuss dies down in Nashville ... and you don't need any more complications in your life.*

'Do come in, Mr O'Neill.'

'I'm sure he's got ... ' Sandi stuttered.

'It'd be my pleasure.' He stepped inside before she could come up with an excuse to stop him.

'I've made a couple of spare pasties. Stay and have your tea with us,' Mrs. Thomas offered. 'As a thank you.'

Kieran gave Sandi's mother his broadest, most charming smile. 'I'd sure love to.' *Game on.*

6

Sandi lay back on the sofa, where she'd been ordered to put her feet up, and watched the rest of her family come under Kieran's spell. Of course, Pip already thought he was a red-headed god, and now her mother and father fell for his easy-going ways. By the time he'd told them about life in Nashville, played Snakes and Ladders with Pip, and praised her mother's cooking to the skies, Sandi had to admit she'd lost this particular battle.

Suddenly he glanced her way and winked. Despite her best efforts, Sandi's cheeks burned, and she damped down the dangerous thoughts flying around her head. The ones that said she was twenty-nine, not ninety, and maybe a little fun in her life would make a welcome change ...

Sandi shifted her focus back on Pip. The idea of hurting him wasn't an option.

'Pip. It's time to go. Say goodbye to Mr. O'Neill, and give Nana and Grandpa a kiss.' Sandi ignored her mother's quizzical stare. Pip tried to protest, but she gave him the special look that told him not to argue. 'Make sure you've got your school bag.'

'I'll give you both a lift.' Kieran jumped up before she could protest. 'Thank you for inviting me to share your meal, and for your company.' He grinned at her mother. 'You've won me over to the virtues of the pasty.'

'You make sure to come and see us anytime. I don't like to think of you up there in that big house on your own.'

Sandi mentally rolled her eyes. Anyone would think Kieran was a nervous teenage girl instead of a muscular, six-foot-plus man who could plainly take care of himself.

'I'll be taking you up on that,' he declared. 'Come on. Let's get you two on home.'

In the car, Pip chattered non-stop, saving Sandi from having to make polite

41

conversation. As soon as the car came to a halt, she got out and opened the back door for her son.

'There's no need for you to see us in. We'll be fine.' She hurriedly backtracked, knowing she'd sounded rude: 'I really appreciate all your help. I'll see you in the morning.'

'Be a good boy for your mom, Pip.'

'I'm always good,' he giggled. 'Bye, Mr. O'Neill.'

Sandi met Kieran's amused gaze and couldn't help smiling back.

'Come on, Mummy,' Pip urged and raced towards their front door.

'No rest for the wicked.' Sandi hoisted her bag up on her shoulder.

'Take care of yourself.'

The genuine kindness in his voice touched Sandi, and she swallowed hard, only able to nod before she limped away.

★   ★   ★

Kieran sighed and drove off before he made some other unwise comment. He'd watched Sandi's disconcertment grow as he got on well with her parents and Pip — but she'd got his motives wrong. He'd genuinely enjoyed feeling part of a family again.

He hadn't seen much of his own parents over the last few years because he'd been so tied up with work, and his mother's big lottery win at Christmas hadn't helped matters. Every time he phoned her, conversation revolved around the latest designer clothes she'd bought, or the fancy bathroom she'd had installed with its spa shower and built in sound system. He knew she'd had a hard life up until a few years ago, when his own musical success meant he could make things easier for his parents, but the change in her still bothered him. His quiet father never said much, but Kieran had picked up that all wasn't well between his parents.

He pulled into the driveway at *Gwel an Mor* and got out of the car. He ignored the house and wandered down through the untidy garden until he reached the crumbling wall overlooking the cliff and its sheer drop down to the beach. He breathed in the heady scent of honeysuckle drifting in the breeze, humming under his breath, tapping his fingers against his thigh in a persistent rhythm. The same tune had been running through his head for days, and now lyrics of regret and hope filled his brain until he knew he'd go crazy if he didn't write them down. He hurried back to the house and impatiently unlocked the door, rushed into the study, and pulled his fiddle from its case. After a rudimentary tuning, he began to play, and time disappeared.

A painful twinge in his shoulder made Kieran stop mid-phrase, and he straightened his back, giving it a satisfactory crack. Glancing out of the window, he wondered if there was a storm brewing, because the sunlight had disappeared, leaving a dark, moody sky behind. He looked at his watch and checked it again. How did it get to be nine o'clock? The scrawled sheets of music he'd written lay all around him on the floor, and he'd need to organise them later before starting to lay down the first recording.

He pulled up short. For nearly a year he'd managed to stay away from his music; but now, for whatever reason, hadn't been able to resist a moment longer. Of course, this didn't mean he *had* to do anything with it ... Who was he fooling? Ever since he wrote his first song at the tender age of nine, it'd been a compulsion — some would say an addiction — but it was one he'd never wanted to be cured of. At least, until Helen ruined everything ...

Kieran rubbed a hand idly over his bristly, unshaven chin, and decided that leaving Nashville hadn't been such a terrible idea after all. A snapshot of Sandi and Pip filled his head, and he didn't try to push it away. He subscribed to the theory that everyone who appeared in a person's life did so for a reason.

He glanced around the room. He'd banished Sandi from cleaning in here because he had no intention of explaining the accumulation of guitars and recording equipment to her or anyone else. Being anonymous was a relief after the media scrutiny he'd gone through recently.

A persistent ringing sound penetrated his consciousness, and he realised it was the old-fashioned telephone in the hall. Kieran carefully placed his fiddle on the chair and wandered out of the room.

'O'Neill.' He caught a quick intake of breath before the distinct click of a phone being hung up. There was probably a number he could call to check who it might've been, but Kieran couldn't be bothered right now. He'd fix himself a quick mug of coffee and get back to work. *Back to work.* That sounded good.

* * *

Sandi paced up and down her tiny kitchen, and wished she could get her mother's words out of her head.

Pip keeps asking me about his dad. You need to tell him about Mike. You're usually a straight-spoken girl.

She'd been a mess when Pip was

a baby — guilty and tearful over her failed marriage, and nervous of trying to raise her son alone. When Pip started to ask questions, she'd simply avoided answering him, and told herself there would be time enough later.

'Mummy, I'm ready for my story,' Pip shouted from his bedroom, and Sandi made up her mind to stop being a coward.

'I'm coming.' On the way out of the kitchen, she grabbed two bars of chocolate. They'd need them.

7

'Is your knee still poorly?' Pip frowned as Sandi tucked the covers in around him.

'Not really. It's a bit sore, that's all.' She stroked his soft red hair. 'Granny said you asked about your daddy tonight.' Sandi felt awful as his eyes filled with tears. 'Would you like to see a picture of him?'

She reached down the small album she'd brought in with her, and encouraged Pip to move over so she could slide into the bed next to him. Her throat tightened as she opened the first page and saw her wedding photo. Only seven years ago on the calendar, but it might as well have been in another lifetime.

'He's got my hair!' Pip exclaimed.

'Yes, he has, my sweet.'

'What's his name?'

Sandi bit back tears. 'Mike. Mike Tregonning.'

'Why doesn't he live with us?'

48

As gently as she could, Sandi explained, and watched Pip trying to make sense of her words. 'He loved you very much.' When they separated, Mike had thought it better not to confuse Pip by visiting too soon — but he'd never asked to see his son again. Her mother didn't understand why she'd only used Mike's maintenance money when she was absolutely desperate, and saved the rest in the bank for Pip. Sandi had been determined to prove she could manage alone.

He snuggled down into her arms and she inhaled his clean, little-boy scent.

'How about we eat our chocolate while I read a story?'

'Okay, Mummy.'

Her mother had been right. Pip was only six, and he'd just needed reassurance, not a long-drawn-out explanation. From now on, she could tell him snippets of information until he formed a mental picture of his father that he could deal with.

'I want a King Arthur story tonight,' Pip declared with a big grin.

'Perfect choice.' Reading a story about a knight rescuing a damsel in distress, she could do.

⋆   ⋆   ⋆

Excitement flowed through Kieran's veins and left him more alive than he'd been in years. He was exhausted and starving, but that didn't matter. After he'd laid down a rough version of the first song, his inspiration had continued to flow long past sunrise.

It was too late now for a bath and change of clothes before Sandi arrived for work. He needed a caffeine infusion. Filling up the new coffee maker he'd bought, he turned it on and leaned against the counter, idly looking out over the overgrown back garden. He decided to ask Sandi if she could recommend someone from the village to tackle the mess.

The phone jangled in the hall, and he let it ring. Everyone he was bothered about hearing from knew his mobile number, and could call that instead. After a while,

50

whoever it was gave up, and in the silence he heard the echo of the doorbell and a key rattling in the lock. He'd given Sandi a key in case he was ever out when she came here to work.

'Mr. O'Neill? Are you here?' She poked her head in around the kitchen door.

The urge to celebrate his reinvigorated enthusiasm for music with someone was almost overwhelming, but logic reared its sensible head and he held back.

'I certainly am. Sorry about that. I didn't hear the doorbell.'

'Probably because the phone was ringing.'

'Yeah, well, I'm a popular guy.'

'Answering it usually helps.'

He ignored the pithy comment and offered her coffee instead. 'Fresh-ground beans. The real stuff.' Kieran smiled. 'I've got a box of Cornish gingerbreads as well.'

'Be still, my beating heart.' The hint of a smile tugged at her lips. 'First a Hoover, and now biscuits! You certainly know how to spoil a lady.' As soon as the words left Sandi's mouth, her cheeks turned bright red.

'I do my best.' He enjoyed the moment of fun. All too soon, she'd slip back into serious, responsible mode, and that would be it for the day. 'Are you taking me up on my offer? Coffee?'

'Thank you, but I'm here to work.' She scanned down over him. 'Would you like me to do your washing this morning?'

Kieran became aware of his rough appearance, especially to someone who'd obviously scrubbed from head to toe this morning, and whose immaculate white shirt gleamed so brightly it hurt his tired eyes. She plainly thought he was out of clean clothes. 'Thanks, but I'm good. I'll take my coffee upstairs and have a bath.' He strode out of the room before he could be idiotic enough to explain himself.

★　★　★

Sandi couldn't help being curious. Despite his crumpled clothes, tired eyes and the thick stubble darkening his lean face, she'd picked up on an air of suppressed excitement about Kieran. But she must keep her questions to herself and respect his privacy. Losing this job wasn't an option.

The water pipes creaked over her head, and she forced herself back to work. She packed away the groceries he'd asked her to buy, and put together a quiche ready to bake later. Her recipe shouldn't come under the heading of so-called 'girly food' because it had plenty of bacon, sausage, onion and mushrooms, as well as a ton of sharp cheddar cheese and fresh eggs from a local farm.

She got her supplies from the cupboard and prepared to give the hall bathroom a good clean. Another room on today's agenda was a large, sunny lounge overlooking the back garden that she'd persuaded him to let her tackle.

'That's better.'

Sandi hadn't heard any footsteps, but there Kieran was in the doorway: wearing clean clothes, bare feet, and a satisfied smile. From across the room, she caught a hint of his pine soap, and struggled to ignore her racing heart. She didn't *want* to be attracted to Kieran — or any other man.

'I don't suppose you've got any bacon left?'

Focus. 'Certainly. Sit down and I'll cook you some breakfast.' His eyes sparkled, but he did as he'd been told and settled at the kitchen table. 'Fried or scrambled eggs?'

'Fried.'

'Sorry?'

Kieran's teasing smile made her blush. 'The eggs.'

She quickly turned back to the cooker and her shaking hands struggled to open the egg box.

'I'm thinking of going up to Tintagel at the weekend. Would you and Pip like to come along?'

The bacon sizzled in the frying pan, and she turned down the heat while considering how best to reply. 'That's very kind of you, Mr. O'Neill, but we couldn't possibly.'

'Call me Kieran, please.'

She kept her back to him. 'Fine. Kieran. The answer is the same.'

'Why? Isn't Pip interested in King Arthur? I thought he was the other day.'

Her son had been begging to go to Tintagel, but she'd had to keep putting him off because she had so little free time. 'Yes. He is.'

'So what's the problem?'

'Please don't take offence, but I prefer to keep my personal life separate from work.'

He gave a thoughtful nod. 'I understand.'

Sandi had an awful feeling he did. Only too well. She dropped an egg in the hot fat and stopped the conversation.

8

Kieran made a quick retreat from the kitchen after he'd eaten his breakfast, and holed up in the living room. He started to tape together the flat-pack boxes he'd bought the day before, ready to make a start on sorting out the thousands of books. It would take a specialist in old volumes to deal with the rarer ones, but the majority were best taken to the nearest charity shop.

He set up his iPod on the table and turned it on full blast. Humming along to Ed Haley, an old-time West Virginia fiddler, Kieran soon got engrossed.

'Um, excuse me, do you want me to answer the phone?'

He glanced up to see Sandi hovering in the door and gesturing towards the hall. 'Yeah, okay.' Maybe his mystery caller would speak if he didn't answer it himself.

'Sorry. No luck.' She quickly returned. 'I called 1471, but the number was withheld. Probably either a nuisance call or from overseas.'

'No worries.'

She didn't leave immediately, and Kieran took a stab in the dark. 'What'd you think of this music?'

'I didn't mean to overhear, but ... '

'Music's meant to be listened to. No point to it otherwise.' He hit the play button again, and a wide smile lit up her face. 'That's Ed Haley: he was a blind fiddler from Logan County, West Virginia, where I grew up. There're very few original recordings from him, but people are starting to play his music again. In fact, I ... ' Kieran stopped short, unable to admit he'd recorded some himself. 'Do you like it?'

'Very much. It's not unlike some of the traditional Cornish folk songs.'

He could talk for hours on the history of different types of music brought to America by immigrants as a comfort and a way of bringing along their past to their new lives, but it would lead to her asking too many questions. 'Do any of the pubs around here have live music?'

Sandi nodded. 'I used to like going along to listen, but haven't had the chance for a long time.' The fact that her life didn't allow for much in the way of freedom hung between them. 'I'd better go back to work.' She smoothed a hand down over her hair, although there wasn't a strand out of place.

In an effort to keep her talking, Kieran remembered about the garden, and that did the trick for five minutes as they discussed possible options. She agreed to ask a couple of people if they might be interested in the work.

After she left, his concentration for book sorting was shot, but a new song clawed at his brain. Kieran grabbed the pad he'd been writing notes on and scribbled down the rough tune. The shape of the lyrics formed as well, which didn't always happen simultaneously, and he worked frantically to capture them before they disappeared.

'Gosh, you can really sing.' Sandi blurted out. 'Sorry. It's none of my business,' she hurried to apologise. 'I came to tell you lunch is ready.'

It had shocked her to hear Kieran's rich, deep voice filling the room. She turned on her heels and rushed back to the kitchen to splash cold water on her face in an effort to cool her flaming cheeks.

'Hey, it's okay. No need to run off.' Kieran's rumbling voice behind her made Sandi jump. 'I wasn't exactly keeping quiet, was I?' He gently rested his hands on her shoulders and eased her around to face him.

'No. You weren't.' Under his perceptive gaze, she almost forgot how to breathe.

'Keeping our personal and work lives separate isn't always easy, is it?'

'No, but it's sensible.'

'It's a pity I didn't learn that lesson years ago.' By the slight bitterness to his tone, Sandi guessed he was talking about another time and place. 'Lunchtime?'

Sandi nodded, and quietly started to dish up his plate. She poured out a large glass of the sweetened ice tea he'd taught her how to make. 'You might want to take a look at the back sitting room later. It's looking good, if I say so myself.' She rattled on about her plans for the next day while she tidied the kitchen counter. 'I'll see you tomorrow.'

'You will indeed. Thanks again.'

'What for?'

'Everything,' he murmured.

Sandi didn't dare to reply, and without another word she gathered up her basket and left. Outside, she exhaled a relieved sigh and strode off down the road. Thank goodness she had a long shift at the café to work that would keep her from thinking too much about Mr. Kieran O'Neill.

Six exhausting hours later, she acknowledged her foolishness. One spilled teapot. Two mistaken orders. The three times she had to be reminded to empty the bins. Agnes and Mel had exchanged amused smiles at her unusual behaviour.

At least Pip would have had his tea by the time she finally picked him up, meaning she could make do with a bowl of cereal. Normally she looked forward to their evenings together but tonight she'd be counting the minutes until she could get him into bed.

Sandi trudged along the street and made it to Polkirt Street unscathed, which was little short of a miracle considering the day she'd had.

'Mummy!' Pip ran out to meet her, bursting with excitement. 'Come on.' He dragged on her hand.

Everything all right? She mouthed the question to her mother over Pip's head, and Jean shrugged. Before she could ask anything else, a shadowy figure appeared behind her mother's shoulder and stepped out into the early evening sunshine.

'It's my Daddy!' Pip's shrill voice barely pierced the fog swirling around her brain as Sandi tried to get her head around the sight of Mike Tregonning, older and a little heavier around the middle, giving her a tentative smile.

'Long time, no see,' Mike said.

'Come in and have a cup of tea, love.' Her mother came to Sandi's rescue.

'When did Mike turn up?'

'He was waiting outside the school when I went to collect Pip.' Jean managed a half-smile. 'As soon as Pip spotted him, he got so excited.'

Sandi was afraid. She didn't want to see her little boy hurt. She put on a bright smile and braced herself for trouble.

9

She watched Pip sleep, curled in a ball with the covers pulled up over his head so only a few tufts of bright red hair stuck out, and rubbed at the headache throbbing at her temples.

I'm in a better place now, Sandi. I was young and scared and didn't behave well. I treated you and Pip badly, and I want the chance to make amends.

Mike had bought a house nearby and left his father's firm to start his own local building company.

I can help if you'll let me.

She'd made a noncommittal reply until she could think straight again.

I'll give you a ring at the weekend and we can talk.

She'd been on her own with Pip for so long, Sandi didn't know how to feel about Mike's sudden reappearance in their lives. Over the last six years, she'd often wondered how it would feel to see Mike again — but apart from shock and surprise, she'd been oddly unmoved. He wasn't the nineteen-year-old boy she'd fallen in love with, and she certainly wasn't the same girl. For the first time in hours, Sandi's shoulders lost some of the tenseness that had been tying them up in knots.

★　★　★

He'd become a nocturnal animal at this rate. Another frantic writing session had carried through to another sunrise. Kieran yawned and wandered out of the back door for a breath of fresh air. He tried to decide if it was worse to ask Sandi to cook breakfast for him again, or do his own and mess up her tidy kitchen. A smile tugged at his mouth. *Her* tidy kitchen? Whose house was it anyway? Without even saying a word, she'd managed to express disapproval of his slovenly habits, and Kieran found he was tidying up after himself even when she wasn't around. Suddenly he remembered Sandi mentioning the room she'd worked on yesterday.

Kieran wandered down the hall and opened the door, letting out a whistle of approval as he glanced around. He'd been reluctant to let her bother with any other rooms, because his mother intended to pull it all apart when she arrived, but Sandi had been right. The large bay windows, sparkling clean in the sunlight, looked out over the massive sweep of the back garden. After only a few days' work by his new gardener, the original design had started to emerge. The stunning scarlet and white rhododendrons were in full bloom, and even the shabby pergola in the middle of the lawn had an air of faded glory.

He hurried back to the study to fetch his mountain dulcimer. This wasn't an instrument he habitually played, but it'd be perfect for the song filling his head. Resting it on his lap, he began to strum the four simple strings and hum along with the rhythm.

'He plays, too! A man of many talents.'

Kieran turned to see Sandi standing in the doorway.

'You didn't hear me ring the bell again. You shouldn't have given me a key if you wanted to keep your vices a secret.'

'It's hardly a vice,' he retorted. Kieran needed to get away from talking about music with her, because she was too smart to fool for long. 'You've done a great job with this room. You were right.'

'Men don't often tell me that.' Sandi's wry smile disappeared as fast as it'd arrived.

'More fool them.' His impulsive reply brought a flush of heat to her porcelain skin.

'Breakfast?' Her brisk question put them back on their regular footing, and he was relieved.

'Do you mind? It wasn't part of our original deal.'

'You're paying me to work here. If you want me to spend more time cooking and less time cleaning, it doesn't matter to me.'

'Fair enough.'

Sandi started to walk away but suddenly swung back around. 'It's no good. My curiosity is too strong.' She pointed to the oddly shaped wooden instrument he was holding. 'What *is* that?'

Thank goodness. A question he could answer honestly. 'It's a mountain dulcimer, native to Appalachia. It was first used among the Scottish and Irish immigrants, although there's no sign it came from either country originally. There's a resemblance to several instruments traditionally found in Continental Europe. The music historians suspect violins were too hard to make, and so the people designed these instead.' Kieran bit his tongue to stop from rambling on.

'I've never heard of it before. That's fascinating. Thanks.' She rushed off, and he was left staring at the space where she'd been. Would telling her a little of his background really hurt? *Yeah, it would.* She'd drawn a clear line between them and he'd no right to cross it.

Kieran laid the dulcimer on the table and headed for the kitchen where the irresistible aroma of sizzling bacon made his stomach rumble.

'Help yourself to coffee.'

He settled in his favourite seat at the end of the pine table so he could watch her. Economical and quiet in her movements, she was a monument to efficiency.

'How's Pip?'

'He's good.'

Kieran noticed Sandi's tense body language and guessed she wasn't being completely honest. 'Really?'

She gave a brief shrug.

'You wanna talk about it?'

Sandi hesitated and then calmly broke an egg into the frying pan. 'I don't think so.'

'If you change your mind, I'm a good listener. No advice given unless it's asked for.' He sipped his coffee.

'There you go.' She placed a loaded plate in front of him. 'Anything else you need before I get busy on the bathrooms?'

'Nope, I'm good. This looks great. I'm starving.'

'Leave the dishes when you're done. I'll clean up later.'

Kieran had no choice but to agree and let her go — again. Shovelling down a delicious mouthful of bacon and eggs, he smiled to himself. This afternoon, he'd walk down to the village and take Jean Thomas up on her invitation to stop by and visit.

10

After his second scone with lashings of strawberry jam and rich, thick clotted cream, Kieran was stuffed. 'Okay, I'm beat, I give in.' Jean laughed, and he was instantly reminded of the one time he'd seen her daughter relax enough to smile.

He found himself telling Sandi's mother more about himself than he'd intended, and came to the conclusion she was a shrewd woman underneath her affable, easygoing exterior. His efforts to get the conversation around to Pip and Sandi weren't proving as easy as he'd expected.

'Did you say your mum's coming here soon?'

Kieran explained about his mother's plan to improve the house without going into details. He preferred not to think about it, because the longer he stayed, the more he was falling in love with his great-uncle's house.

'I'll look forward to meeting her.' She glanced up at the clock. 'I didn't realise how late it was. It's time I left to collect Pip from school.'

'I'm sorry. I didn't mean to overstay my welcome.' Kieran set his plate and cup back on the tray.

'You haven't. Don't be daft.' Jean smiled. 'Walk down with me. He'd like to see you.' A shadow flitted across her face. 'It might stop him going on about when his dad's coming again.'

'I got the impression Pip's father wasn't around?' She threw him a sharp glance, so like her daughter's it verged on eerie. 'Sorry. I didn't mean to pry.'

'You're not.' Jean sighed. 'Don't you dare tell Sandi I said anything to you about all this or she'll skin me alive.' Briefly, she explained that Mike had reappeared after six years and wanted to be a part of Pip's life. 'It's difficult.'

'I'm sure y'all will help sort it out.'

'We're trying, but you know our Sandi, she's a stubborn girl.'

Tell me about it. She wrote the book on the subject.

'Are you coming with me?' Jean asked.

'Why not?' There were plenty of reasons why he should leave and go home, but Kieran liked the kid and was happy to see him again. 'Okay, lead the way.'

Jean grinned. 'Beware. The sight of you is going to stir up all the young mothers at the school gates. And if you're foolish enough to speak, you'll really be in trouble. They'll all fall for your accent.'

Kieran draped an arm around her shoulders. 'Don't worry. I'll tell them I'm into more mature women.'

She batted his arm away with a peal of laughter. 'I can quite see why you've got my Sandi twisted up in knots.'

'Have I?'

'Oh, yes.' Jean nodded. 'But if you ever repeat that, I'll deny it with my last breath.'

He made a sweeping gesture across his throat. 'I swear. It'll never pass my lips.'

*   *   *

If Pip hadn't been in the room, Sandi would have told her mother what she really thought of her afternoon tea session with Kieran. Pip hadn't stopped enthusing about how impressed the other children were to see and hear a real live American at the school.

'He's got a King Arthur book for me, Mummy.'

'That's nice.' Sandi caught her mother suppressing a smile.

'Can we go to Tintagel with Mr. O'Neill? Please. Please. Please. He's going on Sunday and Granny said you're not working.'

Did she really?

'We'll see.'

Pip's face fell. 'That means no.'

'I didn't say that ... '

A mulish expression darkened his face. "We'll see' *always* means no. I hate you.' Pip ran out of the room, and they heard the back door slam.

Sandi made a move to go after him but her mother touched her arm.

'Leave him be, love. He won't come to any harm in the garden.' She patted the seat next to her on the sofa. 'Sit with me a minute. Your dad will make us another cup of tea.'

'I can't leave him alone when he's upset,' Sandi protested.

'Yes, you can. It won't harm Pip — or you — for once.'

She covered her face with her hands. 'I don't know how to do this. Everything was all right before Mike came back, but he's messed everything up.'

'He is Pip's father.'

Of course, her mother was right, and it was up to Sandi to make it work for her son's sake. 'I know.'

'Two teas.' Her father reappeared and set down two brimming mugs in front of them. 'Do you want me to pop out and see the boy? We'll have one of my man-to-man talks.'

'Thanks, Dad.' He left them to it, and Sandi relaxed enough to ask her mother more about Kieran's visit. She was amazed to hear all sorts of things about him she hadn't known — including the fact that he was a profession musician in Nashville. *Because you've never asked, and choked him off when he tried to talk to you more.*

'I got the impression there was a lot he didn't say, though. Keeps it all inside him. Never a good idea, is it?'

Sandi knew that was aimed at her. They'd had enough discussions over the last six years about her nagging guilt over the failure of her marriage. Despite the fact that Mike had been the one to leave because he couldn't cope with the demands of family life, she still found it hard to accept her part in the whole sad story.

'Uh, Sandi, love … ' Her dad came back into the room. 'I'm sure he's just being naughty and hiding from us, but I can't find Pip.'

'This is why I worry all the time.' Rushing from the room, she barely stopped long enough to grab a torch from the kitchen drawer before heading into the garden. Her parents followed her out, and they all called Pip's name into the fading daylight. The dilapidated shed, the overgrown spot by the compost heap, and the dark corner Pip always avoided because of the prickly holly bush — they checked them all. Tears pressed at Sandi's eyes, but she brushed them away. She needed to think clearly, but it was difficult when the knot of terror wouldn't leave her alone.

'Do you want me to call the police?' Her father's anxious voice betrayed his own growing fear.

'Hang on a second. Let me ring Kieran first.' The thought of her little boy trying to find his way up the hill to *Gwel an Mor* was scary. 'I want to warn him to look out for Pip.' She pulled out her phone and called Kieran's mobile. As soon as she heard his voice, Sandi's control broke.

11

'Take it easy, Sandi.' Kieran couldn't make out what she was trying to say. 'Is something wrong with Pip?' A stab of guilt pierced through him when she explained the little boy was upset about his mother's refusal to endorse the potential visit to Tintagel. 'Hey, I'm real sorry, I shouldn't have brought up the subject again.'

'No. You shouldn't. But it's done now.' Sandy sighed. 'That's the least of my worries.'

'I'll come and help look for him.'

'No. Stay there,' Sandi begged. 'I'm afraid he might come looking for you.'

Kieran thought it was unlikely but didn't say so. He'd scared his own parents on more than one occasion by 'running away', but had always stayed within a few minutes' walk of his house. 'I'll wander around outside and switch all my lights on indoors.' There was a suggestion he needed to make, but Sandi wouldn't like it one bit. 'You might consider calling Pip's father.'

'Why?'

Because he has a right to know, and Pip is more likely to try and track him down. Kieran chose his words carefully, and got the rejection he'd expected. 'Think about it and see what your folks say.'

'My Dad wants to call the police.'

'I think I'd wait another half-hour or so, and scour around some more. My guess is that Pip won't have gone far.' Kieran told her about his own childish attempts to freak out his parents, and got a weak laugh out of her. 'As soon as it got really dark and I got hungry, I'd walk back closer to home and let myself be 'found'.'

'Thanks.'

'What for?'

'Trying to help. I know I'm not good at accepting that.'

'I'd noticed.'

'Seriously, I do appreciate it. I've got to go. I'll ring if ... ' Her voice cracked and he ached to reach down the phone and hug her, to tell her everything would be all right. But he wouldn't insult her by offering false platitudes.

'Yeah, keep me in the loop. And if there's *anything* I can do, just ask.' He rang off and wandered back into the other room, picking the dulcimer up without any real urge to play. He toyed with the strings, but his mind was on Pip. The boy hadn't struck him as physically daring, and he couldn't believe he would stray far. A idea came to him. If he suggested it to Sandi, she'd say he was insulting her intelligence — but Pip's safety was the only thing that mattered now.

* * *

'Have you found him?' Sandi yelled down the phone.

'No, but ... '

'I don't have time to talk. The local policeman just arrived.' The sight

79

of the uniformed constable on her parents' doorstep had about finished her off.

'Give me five seconds. Please.'

The desperate edge to Kieran's voice silenced her.

'Has Pip got his own bedroom at your folks' house?'

'Well, yes, they've always kept one for him.' Sandi couldn't hide her exasperation. 'And yes, of course we've looked in there.'

Kieran gently asked if it had been a casual check, or whether they'd searched every inch of the room. 'After we hung up, I remembered that once I wriggled into the top of my mother's closet behind her handbags and hatboxes, and stayed there until I needed to pee.' He chuckled. 'I clambered down, and my mom was sitting on the bed waiting for me. She'd spotted the toe of my shoe and decided to wait me out.'

'Clever woman.' Sandi reluctantly had to admit they'd only glanced in the room earlier. 'I'll go now and have a thorough look.' She dropped the phone and ran upstairs.

She threw open the door and stopped in her tracks. Instead of giving in to her natural impulse to tear the room apart, she stood still and listened, letting her eyes do the searching. Nothing was obviously out of place. Pip hadn't spent the night here for several weeks, and her mother was a meticulous housekeeper.

A slight bump rose up in the middle of the pale blue quilt, and despite everything, Sandi smiled. Young children had the foolish idea that if they couldn't see someone, the same worked in reverse. Even her intelligent son wasn't immune to that particular fallacy.

She crept across the room and bent down over the bulge in the bed.

'Do you want me to tickle you, Philip Michael Thomas?'

The covers flew up into the air and a red-faced Pip scrambled out of the bed. 'No, Mummy, please. I'm sorry.' Huge, hot tears flooded down his face, and she almost felt sorry for him. Almost.

'You're a very naughty boy.' Pip needed to understand this hadn't been a game. 'A lot of people were worried about you.' His gulping sobs tore at her heart, and she pulled him to her and kissed his sweaty forehead. 'You frightened me. I love you so much, and I thought I'd lost you.'

'I love you too, Mummy.' Pip buried himself in her chest.

Later, they'd have to talk properly, but for now she'd stick with being grateful. For once, Pip allowed Sandi to pick him up and carry him. He wrapped his hot little fingers around her neck, and buried his face in her chest the same way he'd done as a tiny baby.

'Panic over!' Sandi yelled from the top of the stairs as she started to walk down, carefully carrying her precious bundle. 'Safe and sound.' Her parents and PC Treneague rushed out into the hall and their questions flowed thick and fast. She realised she hadn't given a thought to Kieran, without whom they'd still be searching.

'Mum, take care of Pip a minute, please. I must ring Kieran. He'll be worried sick.'

'Of course. We'll go into the kitchen and put the kettle on.' Jean reached for Pip and swapped him over into her arms.

Sandi entered the wrong number the first time, and as soon as Kieran answered, she blurted out the good news. 'I can never thank you enough. I know he'd have been found eventually, but it might have taken hours, and I ... ' She gulped back a sob.

'I know, honey. I wish I was there to ... ' Kieran's voice trailed away.

'To what?'

'Give Pip a big hug.'

She guessed it wasn't what he'd intended to say, but this wasn't the right moment to push.

'Bring Pip with you tomorrow when you come to work. I'd like to see him again.'

Sweet man. He knew she wouldn't want to be parted from her son, but couldn't afford not to work. 'Thank you.'

'You're welcome. And I promise not to mention Tintagel.'

Sandi sighed. 'Good. I've still got to cross that bridge.' She had a lot to deal with, and whether or not to agree to a day out with Kieran was a long way down the list.

12

'How about just for the afternoon instead?' Mike begged, backpedalling on his request to take Pip out for the whole day on Saturday. 'Keri really wants to meet him.'

'Who's Keri?'

'My new wife. Didn't I mention her?'

Sandi bit her tongue before answering in a calm, non-confrontational tone of voice: 'No, you didn't.'

'Could we pick him up at noon and take him out for lunch?'

She didn't want to resent Mike for being happy, but it hurt when he described the beautiful house he'd built for Keri, and the exotic honeymoon they'd spent in Bali last year. All she'd got had been a damp flat in Watford and a weekend in Blackpool.

'Pip's a bit fussy about what he eats. Nothing green. The food on his plate can't be touching. No gravy. He won't eat sausages either, or anything he can't recognise.'

'What about a pasty?'

'Only the ones my Mum makes. He won't touch a shop one.'

Mike sighed. 'We'll find something for him. Don't worry.' He cleared his throat. 'I know I can never make up to Pip or you for leaving the way I did, but it's not going to stop me trying.'

The earnest pleading in his gruff voice got to her.

'Okay. Pick him up from Mum and Dad's at noon, and bring him home no later than five.'

'Thanks. I can't tell you how much I … ' His voice cracked.

'Look, I need to leave for work. Bye.' She hung up and took several deep, steadying breaths. 'Pip,' she called down the hallway, 'hurry up. We need to go.' Before she had finished speaking, he raced out of the bedroom with his hair sticking up in all directions, a tooth-paste smear on his cheek, and wearing a mismatched assortment of clothes. His offbeat combination of a red t-shirt, orange-and-white shorts and thick green cardigan, worn with black flip-flops and knee-length blue-and-white striped socks, was *so* Pip she had to smile. No doubt he'd raced through the list of things she'd told him to do before sticking his head back into whatever book was fascinating him today.

'Remember what I ... '

'I know, Mummy.' She stifled a grin as he rolled his eyes. 'Be polite. Behave. Don't talk too much. Don't touch any of Mr. O'Neill's things unless he says I can.' The sing-song way he repeated her words was priceless, but Sandi kept a straight face. The swirl of fear returned, and she wanted to clutch him tightly to her. What if last night had ended differently?

Sandi put on a bright smile. 'Let's go.'

★   ★   ★

Kieran didn't comment on the dark shadows under her eyes, but instead focused his attention on Pip. 'How about you come with me and take a look through my great-uncle's old books? If we're lucky, we might find something on King Arthur, because he enjoyed reading about him too.'

'He doesn't need to bother you,' Sandi intervened. 'Pip can come with me while I work and read quietly in the kitchen.'

The boy's face fell, and Kieran ached for him. 'He wouldn't be a bother. I don't have anyone else who shares my interest.' Sandi glanced between the two of them. 'I'll keep a close eye on him. You don't have to worry.' Her pretty blue eyes softened. For once, he'd said the right thing. 'Are orange squash and chocolate-chip cookies allowed?'

'I didn't realise you were a squash drinker?' Sandi teased.

'It's not bad stuff.' He couldn't help grinning. 'I'd always *eaten* my squash before, so this is a novelty.'

'That's silly. You can't eat squash.' Pip giggled. 'I suppose you could freeze it and make ice cubes and eat them. That would work.'

Smart kid. 'It would, but I'm talking about a vegetable that grows where I come from in America.'

'I don't like vegetables. Except carrots,' Pip declared.

'I'll do you a deal.' The boy gave him a wary look. 'You can take any of my books home with you to read if you promise to try my sort of squash. I cook it real good — sliced and dipped in cornmeal, and then fried. It's like candy.' Kieran held out his hand. 'Remember, a man's handshake is important. It's a promise he never breaks.' Over the boy's shoulder, he caught a hint of approval on Sandi's face.

'I'll eat one bite.'

'Three,' Kieran countered.

'Two.' Pip grasped his hand and their eyes met. The serious way the little boy shook his hand was priceless.

'I tracked some squash down in Truro a couple of days ago at the market, so we can have it for lunch today.'

'But we've got to … '

He quickly cut off Sandi's objection.

'Is there anywhere you *have* to be before one o'clock?'

'Well, no.'

'In that case, Pip and I are cooking lunch today. You can get on with your work, and we'll have it ready for noon. Sound good, buddy?'

'I'm not sure it's a good idea,' Sandi interrupted before Pip could reply. 'You'll have hot oil, and … '

'We'll be careful, I promise. Everyone, man or woman, needs to be able to take care of themselves.'

'I thought you couldn't cook?' she persisted.

'I never said that.'

'The implication was there.'

'Two totally different things, honey.' Kieran wasn't going to let her win this one. He didn't blame her for being protective, but Pip needed to be allowed to spread his wings.

'Fine.' Sandi threw her hands in the air. 'I'll get on with my work. You asked for him. You've got him.' She fixed a stern stare on Pip. 'Remember what we talked about before we came.'

'Yes, Mummy.' His obedient answer was at odds with the broad smile lighting up his face.

Kieran steered the boy out of Sandi's reach before she could issue any additional warnings. 'We'll go upstairs. There are a ton of books in my uncle's bedroom I haven't looked at yet.' Pip instantly raced away, leaving him to try and keep up.

As soon as he opened the door, Pip squeezed in past.

'Wow!' Excitement bubbled out of him at the sight of hundreds of books crammed into every possible space, barely leaving enough room for the furniture.

'You start on that side,' Kieran pointed, 'and I'll try over here.' Another day, he'd do a more organised search, but this would keep Pip occupied. Bending down, he pulled out books from under the bed and started to look through them. After a while, he sneaked a quick peek at Pip to see him sitting cross-legged on the floor and methodically checking through a pile of what looked like encyclopaedias.

Suddenly, Pip jumped up. 'Mr. O'Neill, look! King Arthur.' He raced over and thrust a book in Kieran's face. 'It's got cool pictures.'

The cover was a spectacular illuminated scene of an austere King Arthur sitting at the famous Round Table, surrounded by his knights. 'Let's take a break and look at it.'

That was the last sorting they got done.

★ ★ ★

If she scrubbed the bath any harder, the enamel surface would come off. There was a lot of banging coming from the kitchen, and she dreaded to imagine what sort of state it'd be in when they'd finished. Pip's childish giggles and Kieran's deep, warm rumbling laughter echoed through the house. *You could go and join them. You could have fun too.* The only times she'd really let go of her emotions was in her art — and in her wild teenage love for Mike. She was far more cautious now.

Sandi wiped the tub dry before putting away everything in her box of cleaning supplies. Now she had to sit at a table with Kieran and eat and make polite conversation. From day one, he had ignored her attempt to keep him at arms' length. She crept downstairs and stowed her supplies in the cupboard, before sneaking into the guest bathroom to give her hands a good wash. Checking her appearance in the small mirror, she tidied back a few rogue strands of hair.

She braced herself to face the lunch-time music.

13

'Did the good cooking smells lure you to quit work?' Kieran said.

She glanced at her watch. 'It is twelve o'clock.'

'Yep, I know. I was funning you.'

'Oh, right.' A tight smile played around her lips, but she didn't give into it.

Kieran pointed to a chair and put on his best stern expression. 'Sit.'

'I could … '

'Nope,' he interrupted, 'you aren't going to do a thing. My trusty assistant will take your order.' He nodded at Pip, hovering by his side with a notepad and pencil clutched in his hands. They'd tied a white cloth around his waist to resemble a waiter's apron and protect his clothes from getting messed up. Kieran guessed the kid had picked out the motley collection himself this morning, because no way would the immaculate, well-groomed Sandi have chosen such a random selection. Of course, he had no room to criticise, because his own ragged athletic shorts and ancient high school t-shirt had definitely seen better days.

'Mummy. This is the menu. May I fetch you a drink to start with?' Pip frowned in deliberate concentration. 'You can have water or orange squash.'

'Water, please.'

'Are you ready to order?'

Kieran glanced over his shoulder and watched Sandi study the handwritten menu. She asked several questions, and Pip recited the list of ingredients and how everything was cooked.

'I think I'll have the baked haddock with fried squash, broccoli and home-made bread rolls.' She raised an eyebrow in Kieran's direction.

Pip wasn't lying. Kieran's grand-mother had taught him how to make her famous cloverleaf rolls, and he'd had a craving for them the other day.

'Are you both joining me?'

'Of course.' Pip giggled. 'You'd be

lonely on your own.'

'I certainly would.' Sandi's eyes shone with pride as they rested on her son.

Kieran fought against giving into laughter when the little boy walked over and repeated his mother's order word for word. He started to help dish up their lunch.

'Do I *have* to try that too?' Pip turned up his nose at the bowl of sautéed broccoli.

'Yeah. It's rude not to eat some of everything when you have guests.'

With a sigh, Pip dropped one floret on his plate. 'And this?' He pointed to the crispy fried squash. 'Two, right?' Their agreement hadn't been forgotten.

'Yep.' Kieran lifted the tray of fish out of the oven and set it on the counter. He passed the spatula to Pip and ignored Sandi's frown as he guided the boy's hand, sliding it under the first portion and lifting it up and onto her plate. 'You okay with carrying this, buddy?'

Pip nodded, and grasped it with both hands before taking small, measured steps over to the table. He placed it down in front of his mother, and Kieran exhaled the breath he'd been holding.

* * *

Sandi winced inwardly on hearing how much Pip had done to help prepare lunch, from slicing the squash to kneading the bread dough.

'Mummy. Mr O'Neill's fish didn't have fingers.'

Sandi didn't dare to look at Kieran.

'It had a head, and all sorts of nasty bits inside we had to clean out. I didn't want to touch it, but Mr. O'Neill said if I was going to be a real cook I couldn't be squea-...I can't remember the word; it wasn't 'squeaky'.'

'Do you mean 'squeamish'?' she suggested with a smile, and Pip nodded. Sandi took a bite and couldn't believe how good it was. 'It's delicious.' She tried not to show her amazement as Pip ate his fish without complaint. He stabbed the broccoli with his fork, giving it a silent glare before popping it into his mouth and chewing thoughtfully.

'It's okay.' He looked at Kieran's plate. 'Are you going to eat all of yours?'

'Help yourself.'

'But it's green, and you don't eat green!' Sandi blurted out before she could stop herself.

'It's all in the way it's cooked, isn't it, buddy?' Kieran gave a self-satisfied smile as her son reached over and stabbed a couple more stalks of broccoli, returning them to his own plate. 'Amazing what a touch of garlic, lemon zest and juice, and a spot of soy sauce can do to a dreary vegetable.'

It's all right for you. I'm the one who has to follow this up. You've dropped me in it. Sandi hated to admit that much of Pip's dislike of certain foods was nothing more than childish boredom.

'How about the squash?' Kieran asked, spearing a couple of the crunchy slices. 'In the South, we have the theory anything is better breaded and fried.'

'You're probably right. Unhealthy. But

right.' She mitigated the sharp remark with a smile, and received a teasing one from him in return.

'It's good,' Pip declared. 'Better than the drink.'

They all laughed together, but out of the blue Sandi's eyes burned with unshed tears. The warm atmosphere reminded her of childhood meals with her parents around the kitchen table at number fifty-seven Polkirt Street. This was what things could have been like if she and Mike had been able to hold their own family together.

Kieran squeezed her hand and the comfort of his strong, warm fingers worked wonders. 'Isn't it funny how so many of our memories are connected with food?' In his slow, easy drawl, he sucked her in, spinning a story about his grandmother who'd baked the same bread roll recipe every Sunday and holiday. 'The grown-ups would tell us kids not to fill up on rolls and spoil our meal, but we thought that was the dumbest thing we'd ever heard. Who cared about eating dry old turkey when we could stuff ourselves with Maw-Maw's rolls?' He picked a roll off the top of the basket and held it to her lips. 'Eat. No one can stay sad long when these are around.'

She obeyed and took a large bite, sighing her pleasure through the mouthful of warm, yeasty roll. When she was finished, Kieran brushed away a couple of stray crumbs from her cheek. The phone out in the hall started its insistent ring, and Sandi relaxed back in the chair as he got up to answer it.

★   ★   ★

'Stop pestering me!' Kieran yelled.

'Don't be mad. Please, Kee.'

Kieran didn't know how he remained standing. *Helen.*

'Are you still there?' she continued.

'Yeah.' *But I don't know why.* This last year had been sheer torture. He'd lost the woman who'd broken his heart along with his music. 'Why are you calling?'

'I needed to talk to you.'

He couldn't imagine why. They had nothing left to say to each other.

'You didn't give me a chance to put things right between us before you left for England,' Helen accused.

You had eleven months. Long enough.

'I get it,' she sniffed. 'You wanted to punish me.'

'It's always about you, isn't it?' he said sadly.

'You never used to be so unkind.'

'Having my love thrown back in my face and my career ruined — let's just say it changed me.' He hoped he'd struck a chord with her. 'I've got things to do. Don't call me again. Goodbye.'

'Don't hang up. Please.' Helen's voice trembled. 'Open the door.'

'What door?'

'Your front door,' she whispered. Kieran walked towards it in a trance. He slipped back the lock and opened the door a couple of inches. 'Surprise.'

14

A woman's voice drifted in from the hall, and Sandi picked up on a hint of shock threading through Kieran's indistinct words.

'Mummy. Where's Mr. O'Neill gone?' Pip asked. 'We made an apple pie and he's got ice cream. He promised I could have caramel sauce with mine, the same as he does. When's he coming back?'

'I'm not sure.' She was certain her son didn't know what caramel sauce was, but because it was a favourite of Kieran's, he now considered it the most desirable thing on the planet. 'How about we start to clean up? We'll have our pudding when he comes back.'

Pip jumped down from his chair. 'I'll tell him to hurry up.' Before she could make him sit back down, he'd disappeared.

'Right, Pip, you start to clear the table.' Kieran walked back in, and his dark brooding eyes were in complete contrast to his cheerful voice. A tall, slender woman stepped into the kitchen behind him. 'This Helen Ross. She's an old … friend of mine.'

The elegant blond with the mile-long legs and white lace skirt short enough to use as a handkerchief must be one of Kieran's reasons for being in Cornwall.

Sandi stuck out her hand and introduced herself. 'Are you on holiday, Miss Ross?'

'Call me Helen.' She tossed the lush mane of hair over one shoulder and her insincere smile didn't fool Sandi for one minute. 'I guess you'd say half-vacation and half-work.'

'Oh, right. I'm Kieran's housekeeper.'

The other woman checked her out. 'I thought you must be.'

Ouch.

'Helen's not staying, are you?' Kieran's forceful tone startled Sandi.

'I haven't decided yet. It depends.'

'On what?'

Helen rested her hand on his arm.

'You.'

The awkward silence was broken by Pip, who begged to be allowed to fetch the ice cream from the freezer.

'Sure, buddy.' He threw Sandi a beseeching look and she took pity on him.

'Take a seat, Helen, and I'll clear the table. Would you like a cup of coffee?'

'Black. No sugar.'

Pip beamed at them all. 'I'm going to take the pudding orders.'

Helen winced as he offered her apple pie with any combination of ice cream, caramel sauce and clotted cream. Sandi guessed she was calculating the calorie content on the spot.

'Nothing for me; thanks anyway, kid.'

Her son's face fell and Sandi tried to make up for Helen's curt reply by telling Pip he could put everything on hers. While she got busy tidying up, the American woman watched her every move.

'You've done enough.' Helen patted the chair next to her. 'Sit down so we can get to know each other.'

Kieran kept his back to them and started to dish up the apple pie. So much for helping each other out.

★ ★ ★

He realised it was cowardly, but if Helen was prying into Sandi's background then she couldn't bug him. Kieran hadn't got over the shock of seeing his old love standing on his doorstep. As her music shifted from country to pop, she'd changed her look, and her new glossier style of beauty left him cold. From the perspective of time, he recognised that Helen's behaviour had saved him from making the worst mistake of his life. He'd got carried away and mixed up the good way they made music together with real love.

Pouring out three mugs of coffee, he delivered them to the table along with their desserts. The flash of annoyance Sandi threw his way made him regret his cowardly behaviour. Kieran could've hugged the little boy for being oblivious to the undercurrents in the room as Pip chattered about the crabs he'd caught in a rock pool on the beach yesterday.

'That was delicious,' Sandi declared, putting down her spoon. 'We must be on our way now. Would you like me to wash up?'

'Nope. I'll handle it. I expect you've got things to do.'

'Always.' A faint smile lightened her face. 'I'll see you tomorrow.'

'Bring Pip again.'

'Thank you, but no.' Sandi shook her head, stopping the boy's instant protest. 'He'll be at Mum and Dad's in the morning while I'm here, and then he's going out with his father for the afternoon.'

'Thanks for everything.' Kieran held her gaze for a few precious moments, until a tinge of colour brightened her cheeks and she glanced away. One day soon, he'd explain to her about Helen and his music. 'Pip, don't forget to take the book you found with you.' He glanced at Sandi again. 'Pip's a good detective.

He discovered a cool old book about King Arthur up in Peter's bedroom. I'm afraid we didn't get much more sorting out done afterwards. I told him he could borrow it. It's kind of an adult book, so he'll need some help, but it's got plenty of neat pictures.' Kieran crouched down to Pip's level. 'Next time you come and visit, bring the book with you and I'll take a turn reading it.' He opened his arms wide. 'Do I get a hug?'

Pip wrapped his thin arms around Kieran's neck and wriggled into him. 'I won't forget, Mr. O'Neill . . . ' He stopped talking and let go, staring gloomily at the floor.

Tintagel. He wanted to ask about going to Tintagel. There was nothing Kieran could do. He let Sandi take hold of her son's hand and lead him away. Now it was time to face Helen.

*   *   *

'Why don't we go and sit somewhere else more conducive to talking?' Helen suggested.

Kieran gestured at the detritus of their lunch. 'What about all this?'

'I didn't come all this way to watch you wash a pile of dishes.'

Talk about two very different women. Sandi would have insisted on helping, and had it all done before he could blink.

'Why *did* you come?'

She avoided his gaze and wandered over to stare out of the window. 'Pour me a glass of wine and I'll tell you.'

His stomach churned. Kieran didn't want to hear any more of Helen's excuses.

15

All Sandi wanted to do was go home and lie down in a quiet, dark room and think, but there was no chance of that happening this side of Christmas.

'Mummy, I want you to come too when I go out with Daddy tomorrow.'

When they'd spoken about it before, she'd tried to convey how much fun Pip would have, and been encouraging about the fact his father was keen to spend time with him. 'Darling, I can't. I have to work.'

'Then I'm not going.'

'But you can tell your dad and Keri all about the lunch you helped Mr. O'Neill to cook. And you could take the King Arthur book to show them, if you promise to be very careful with it.' She watched him waver. 'We could make pizza when you come home.'

'With tomato and cheese. Nothing else.'

'Okay,' Sandi conceded, because it wasn't important enough to argue over. 'How about a game of Snakes and Ladders?' Pip beamed. That should take his mind off fretting about his first proper visit with his father, and everything else could wait until he was tucked up in bed. She'd get her laptop out later and do the one thing she'd resisted ever since laying eyes on Kieran. Even if he was only a low-level musician in Nashville — and something made her doubt that — there'd be things out there on the internet about him. She would be patient a little longer.

⋆ ⋆ ⋆

Sandi stared at the screen in disbelief. To say it hadn't been difficult to track down information on Kieran was an understatement. A sick knot formed in her stomach.

Kieran 'Kee' O'Neill, Grammy-winning Americana songwriter and champion of West Virginia roots music, walking the red carpet with his cowriter and girlfriend, renowned mandolin player Helen Ross.

He looked very different clean-shaven, with his rich red hair cut in the kind of studiedly casual way that cost a fortune. His jeans weren't the genuinely old ones she was used to seeing him wear, but artfully faded and full of deliberate holes in an expensive designer way.

Sandi typed in Helen's name. She barely got a mention until five years ago when she'd teamed up with Kieran to write. In the last year, she'd changed genres and released a pop album. The reviews were scathing.

She sipped on her wine and tried a new search, taking a gamble on the fact that whatever had gone wrong between Kieran and Helen had happened fairly recently.

Oh, Kieran. She read page after page of damming stories, and tears trickled unnoticed down her face. The media loved nothing better than to tear down the very people it had built up in the first place. Helen had made a claim that, instead of cowriting Keiran's biggest hit song, it had been written solely by her. In the end, his publisher had settled the case out of court and given Helen a massive payout. Kieran had been dropped by his record label and become a pariah in Nashville. Nothing could persuade Sandi he'd been guilty — but it was no wonder he'd escaped to Cornwall and wasn't inclined to talk.

Sandi closed down her computer, but couldn't stop thinking about Helen's sudden appearance today. What was the woman doing in Penarth? She'd give anything to be a fly on the wall in Kieran's house tonight.

★　★　★

'Write together again? Are you mad?' Kieran exclaimed.

Helen's smile didn't falter. 'I don't expect you to say yes tonight. Think about it.'

'I don't even need five seconds. The answer is a flat-out no. Isn't your new music working out well?'

'I wouldn't say that.'

'I would, honey.' Despite his best efforts, he hadn't been able to resist reading the reviews and following the sales numbers on Helen's new album. 'Abysmal' didn't come close to describing the failure of *Stranger in Music City*. On a low day, he'd even bought a copy and listened to it over and over again — unable to reconcile the canned, clichéd songs with the genuinely heartfelt music she'd made before, both with and without him.

'My manager thinks we need a change of pace. He's suggesting I do a crossover album to tap into the fans I had before …'

'Before you got greedy?' That was what it had all been about. Greed. Pure and simple. Half of the money and credit hadn't been enough for Helen. In the process, she'd ruined his reputation without a second thought. No one in Nashville would touch him with a twenty-foot bargepole, let alone a ten-foot one. Integrity was everything where the music industry was concerned, and the one golden rule was to give credit where it was due. The fact that he hadn't, legally speaking, been found guilty made no difference — the fact that his label agreed to the settlement said it all in other people's eyes.

Helen paled and shifted in her seat. 'I sure am sorry. I never meant for any of this to happen.'

Kieran couldn't let himself feel any sympathy for her.

'I'm not the only one this could help.' She dropped in the throwaway comment and let it hang between them. 'Don't you think it might open the door for you to get back into favour on Music Row?'

There'd been so many dark days over the last year that the small glimmer of light was a tempting prospect, but before agreeing to something he'd regret, Kieran needed to do some serious thinking.

'I think it'd be best if you leave now.'

'You'll think about my offer?' she asked. 'Is there somewhere in the village

I can get a room for the night?'

'There's the White Hart pub, and plenty of bed-and-breakfast places. If you come back here around half-nine in the morning, we'll talk again.'

'Fair enough.' Helen shrugged and stood up. 'Maybe your cute little house-keeper will fix us breakfast.'

Judging by the unimpressed expression on Sandi's face when she met Helen, he wouldn't care to risk his life by asking such a dumb question. No matter how much she wanted this job, Sandi had her limits.

'Breakfast isn't part of her job description.'

'I think she's got her eye on you. A handsome, rich American? Very tempting. You want to watch out.'

'Don't be unkind. Sandi's a hard-working woman who's doing the best for her son and doesn't have an easy life,' he explained. Even if Jean Thomas was right about Sandi's interest in him, Kieran's financial status would be considered a drawback to such an independent woman. 'As far as she's concerned, I'm simply getting my great-uncle's house sorted. Sandi knows almost nothing about my other life.'

'Oh, Kieran.' Helen rolled her eyes. 'Do you really think she hasn't checked up on you, if only to make sure she wasn't coming to work for an axe-murderer?'

Was she right? He couldn't ask Sandi, because it would open up a whole can of worms he had no intention of discussing with her anytime soon.

'I thought you were leaving.' He kept his expression neutral, and she eyed him closely before giving a brief nod.

'Sure am.'

Kieran moved to open the front door and didn't say another word as she joined him. A local taxi was parked outside, saving him from having a wrestle with his conscience about whether to offer her a lift into Penarth.

'I'll see you in the morning.' She kissed his cheek before leaning in close and whispering in his ear, 'Remember how good we were together, Kee dear.'

Kieran stepped back and remained silent as she walked away. As the car drove off, he knew he'd made a huge mistake by not sending her away for good while he had the chance.

16

Sandi's nerves jangled as she strode up the hill to *Gwel an Mor*. She'd given her mother strict instructions to remind Mike of their agreement when he came, and to make sure he brought Pip back by five o'clock. Part of her was relieved she wouldn't have to face Mike today, but her natural curiosity yearned to see what the second Mrs. Tregonning was like.

At the front door she hesitated, took a couple of deep breaths, and forced a smile before ringing the doorbell.

'Hi.' Helen Ross opened back the door. 'Come in.' The woman lounged against the doorway as though she belonged there, and Sandi squashed down a flash of jealousy.

'Thank you.' She stepped inside and headed straight for the kitchen. 'Would you care for some breakfast?'

'Kee said you didn't do breakfast.'

Why would he do that? 'I don't always, but I'm happy to if you're hungry.'

'I'm starving. We worked up an appetite ... '

'...working.' Kieran came to join them. 'We've been working on some music. Helen stayed at the pub last night, and came here early to discuss some business possibilities.'

Sandi didn't make any response, and hoped she gave the impression of being unconcerned. She told them the possible breakfast options, and turned on the coffee pot while she waited for them to decide.

'Black coffee. A two-egg-white omelette with one slice of wheat toast.' Helen rattled off her order as if she was in a hotel. 'Maybe I'll allow myself a strip of bacon this morning, too.'

If that was what she ate when starving, Sandi dreaded to imagine what her normal breakfast consisted of — probably fresh air.

'I'll have the full works, please, if you don't mind.' Kieran's request got raised eyebrows from his ex-girlfriend. 'Can I do anything to help?'

'It's not a problem.'

'He's a big softie, isn't he?' Helen laughed.

There were so many ways Sandi could answer that question, but she simply gave a brief shrug and turned her back on them.

★ ★ ★

Kieran clenched his hands to stop from grabbing Sandi's rigid shoulders and forcing her to look at him. He wished he could spell out exactly what Helen did and didn't mean to him. When he'd stumbled downstairs to answer the door at seven, she'd revelled in his obvious surprise.

Not too early, am I?

Knowing his tendency to sleep late, she'd caught him with his guard down while his brain was still fuzzy from see-sawing back and forth all night. Before he knew where he was, he'd agreed to try

120

working with Helen for a few days and see how things went. When they started to sing together, everything fell back into place as if they'd never been apart — but only as far as the music was concerned. He found it hard to recall how much in love with her he'd thought himself to be. This morning, she'd made several unsubtle attempts to flirt with him, and he'd gently but firmly made it clear that any revival of their personal relationship was off the cards.

'Come and sit down, Kee. Ms. Thomas doesn't need you getting under her feet.' Helen pulled out the chair next to her.

Between Helen's non-stop monologue about the music scene in Nashville, and Sandi's heavy silence as she laid the table and cooked, he retreated into being the Invisible Man. Thankfully, a loaded plate soon appeared in front of him, and gave Kieran the excuse to focus on eating. He always admired Sandi's effortless efficiency when she cooked. *You admire everything she does. Admit it.* Cooking wasn't hard, but when he'd finished working, the kitchen always resembled the aftermath of a nuclear bomb explosion.

He smiled at the fancy extra touches Sandi included on Helen's plate — the artistic smudge of parsley sauce and a fan of perfectly-sliced strawberries.

Kieran wiped up the last of the delicious runny egg yolk with his bread and caught Helen's grimace of disapproval. 'That hit the spot. Thanks, honey.' He gave Helen a fixed stare, and hoped she'd get the hint and show her own appreciation.

'Thanks, Sandi.' She managed two grudging words. 'Are you ready to get back to work?' Helen focused her attention back on Kieran, but he ignored her and spoke quietly to Sandi instead.

'Would you like any help clearing up?

'No, thank you. I know you have a lot of work to do.' Her intonation told him she wasn't impressed by his guest. 'I'll try to stay out of your way and not disturb you with the vacuum.'

This woman had no clue how much she disturbed him on every level. Every day that passed made him long to discover more about the real Sandi, and he couldn't bear the thought of returning to Nashville without having succeeded.

'What are you planning to do today?' He tried to prolong the conversation, seemingly unable to let her go.

'Kee. She's going to clean your house. End of story. Come on.' Helen pushed back her chair and stood up.

Sandi's eyes narrowed as they rested on Helen, and he guessed a few choice words hovered on the tip of her tongue. Reluctantly, he left the room, and sensed her stare on the back of his neck the whole way out.

★ ★ ★

She'd hoped work would do its usual magic and take her mind off Kieran, but so far it was failing miserably. Sandi tried to be objective, but she couldn't work out what he'd ever seen in Helen. The woman was superficially beautiful. Too artificial for her taste — but then, she wasn't a man. She'd listened to Helen's early music — the songs she'd made both before and with Kieran — and it was truly beautiful. Laden with emotion and telling the poignant stories Sandi loved to hear in old folk songs, whether they were from Cornwall or from the other side of the world. It saddened her to see how Helen had changed for the worse, purely from money and a craving for fame.

She needed to face facts. Whether Kieran did or didn't want to rekindle his relationship with Helen should be irrelevant to her. The few times they'd dared to let down their guard had been special; but Sandi had enough on her plate, and so did he. There must be no more wishful thinking.

Saturday was her usual day for changing the sheets and towels, but Sandi found herself strangely reluctant to enter Kieran's bedroom this morning. This was her favourite room because of the superb view. In her mind, she framed a picture out of the window, and wondered if she'd ever paint again. Over the last few weeks she'd thought more about her art than she had since Pip was born. *Was that anything to do with a certain man?* She might get her easel and brushes out again. After all, plenty of people painted as a hobby ...

But it was never a hobby for you. The nagging voice in her head was right. It had been her lifeblood for those few special years. Over time, the longing had faded — but it still lingered, like an unhealed sore place, occasionally itching and burning as a reminder. Between her various jobs and taking care of Pip, there was no time for indulging her own desires: either for art, or for a red-haired man with a slow drawl and an easy smile. They were both out of her reach.

Sandi swung back around and surveyed the messy room. Walking over to the bed, she tugged off the sheets and got back to work.

17

The quiet house wrapped around Kieran and he flopped down on the sofa. Sandi had left with barely a goodbye, whereas he'd practically had to sweep Helen out of the door. When she tried to pressure him on making a decision, he'd continued to hold back. Helen had dropped unsubtle hints about spending the rest of the day together.

Cornwall seems pretty neat and I'd like to explore it some more. Isn't there supposed to be a lively local folk music scene? Maybe we could get lunch somewhere and check out a couple of places. I hear there are some great fish restaurants around this area.

In the end, he'd been firm, and told her that if she didn't stop pestering him, the answer would be a definite *No*. Kieran toyed with the idea of calling his manager to see what Nick thought about Helen's plan, but he didn't want anyone else to make up his mind for him. Nick had sent increasingly persistent emails over the last couple of months, insisting it was time for Kieran to get into serious career-reinvention mode. His manager's suggestions all made sense, but the Nashville music scene had lost its lustre, and Kieran wasn't sure he wanted to be plunged back into the wheeling and dealing that came with being a 'success'.

Idly, he checked his phone and read a few local newspaper articles and entertainment sites relating to a range of popular Cornish folk musicians. An all-male group called 'Smugglers' Secrets' interested him, and he discovered they were performing in a pub in St. Mawes, not far down the coast, tomorrow evening.

Ask Sandi to go with you. The worst she can do is say no. Ever since the first time he'd asked a girl out on a date — when he was thirteen, and Dana, a fourteen year-old heartbreaker, had laughed in his face — Kieran had had an almost pathological fear of being turned down again. The fact that he was now almost thirty-three years old didn't matter. It'd been different with Helen because they'd worked together first, and their personal relationship had grown slowly from there.

Even if he set aside his own pitiful dating history, Kieran knew it wouldn't be easy to break down Sandi's resistance to dating again. He couldn't help thinking that her decision to abandon any notion of a personal life wasn't healthy for her or Pip.

While he gave some more thought to everything filling up his brain, he'd sort through more of his great-uncle's books. Kieran had already hauled several loads off to the nearest charity shop, and found a local book dealer willing to run his eye over what was left. Once the books were done and the house cleaned from top to bottom, there'd be no excuse to put his mother off coming. *Or for you to stay any longer.*

The problem was, Kieran couldn't imagine leaving *Gwel an Mor*. The first day he had walked through the front door, he'd had the crazy but comforting sensation of coming home. The rambling house with its quiet corners, untidy rooms, and pitiful plumbing had welcomed him like an old friend. Kieran wasn't a fanciful man, but he was certain his Great-Uncle Peter somehow approved of his fixation, and he wished he could've known the old man.

He started to put books into piles according to their subjects, and soon a broad smile creased his face. Exercise was important for staying healthy, so he'd take a walk into Penarth later and see if he could catch a certain lady.

* * *

Sandi sighed as she hung up after speaking to her mother. Naturally, Mike had got Pip back on time. She should have guessed he wouldn't give her any reason to complain, and put her illogical resentment down to being overtired. She'd somehow got through the long morning at Kieran's house before coming straight to her shift at the Copper Kettle. Saturdays were always busy in the café, but today's combination of a craft fair in the village hall and good weather meant there were more visitors than usual around Penarth. Her feet and head were aching, and there was still half an hour to endure until closing time. She tried to muster up enthusiasm for the evening ahead, but knowing she had to go home and make pizza before watching Pip's favourite *Camelot* DVD for the umpteenth time wasn't helping her mood.

'Why don't you run on home, love?' Agnes suggested. 'Mel and I can deal with the last few stragglers.'

Sandi hesitated; she'd love to sneak out early, but couldn't afford to lose the small amount of extra money. Pip needed new school shoes, and he'd brought home a letter yesterday about an upcoming class trip to the Eden Project. It all added up — and this month's electric bill had been higher than she'd anticipated. The idea of asking Mike for help stuck in her throat.

'Your pay packet's already made up.' Agnes fished around in her apron pocket and held the envelope out to Sandi. Her tactful compassion brought tears to Sandi's eyes, and forced her to stare down at the floor until she could collect herself enough to take the money from her boss's hand.

'Thanks. Bye, Mel,' she called over to the other waitress who was busy cleaning the display cabinet. Gathering up her basket, she hurried out of the back door. Her first breath of the salty, sun-laden air made the hassles of the day fade away. Nobody would expect her for another half-hour, so she'd wander slowly along by the harbour before making her way up the hill.

'We can't keep meeting like this, honey.'

Sandi swung around and her head hit the middle of Kieran's broad chest. Before she could step back, he clasped her elbows to keep her in place. His dark red hair blew in the breeze, and with a smile he reached up to brush it out of his face.

'My mother keeps nagging me to get it cut. I guess it'd be sensible, but ... '

'Oh, please don't,' Sandi exclaimed, 'it'd be a shame.' Her cheeks burned, and she prayed for an Arctic cold front to swoosh through Cornwall.

'And why is that?' Amusement laced through his voice and reached his glittering eyes.

'You've got attractive hair. That's all,' she muttered, and stared straight ahead at the small rip in his shirt. 'Stop embarrassing me.'

'Wouldn't dream of it.'

Not much, you wouldn't.

'Are you playing hooky? I thought you didn't finish until half-past?'

She was proud of herself for answering his questions sensibly without turning into a teenage girl with a hopeless crush.

'Good. You deserve a break. I fancied a walk, and was going to drop into the café, but now I've gotten to fancying one of those ice creams.' He gestured towards the mobile van parked on the other side of the road. 'Join me. My treat.'

'Thanks, but I can't.'

'Why not?'

'It'll spoil my dinner. I'm cooking pizza for Pip after I pick him up from Mum and Dad's.'

He scoffed. 'Heck. Listen to yourself. You sound like an old woman. Eat less pizza!'

Sandi swallowed down the angry response she'd almost made, because he was right. Right, but he didn't understand her need to think things through and make responsible choices. 'It wouldn't be fair to Pip. He loves ice cream.'

'I'm sure he does, but I won't tell if you don't. I'll buy him one another day. You're a person in your own right, Sandi, not simply Pip's mother. It doesn't do him any good to martyr yourself.'

'You know *nothing* about being a parent. Don't lecture me.'

'I wasn't ... '

'Yes, you were. You have no idea how hard it's been,' Sandi snapped. 'I've read all about your glamorous Nashville life.' Kieran paled, but she couldn't hold back now. 'Mr. Grammy-Award-Winning Musician. What do you know about struggling? Pip's life depends largely on the choices I make. That's a huge responsibility.'

Kieran folded his arms and fixed her with a penetrating stare. 'It sure is. But I don't accept that Pip will turn into a juvenile delinquent if you eat an ice cream without him.'

He made her sound ridiculous. *Was she?* She'd always ignored her mother's efforts to tell her the same thing.

'I didn't exactly mean it that way.' She tried to backpedal, but his expression didn't alter.

'Next time, get your facts straight as well. Yeah, I've got money. I'm sorry about that, but I did work hard for it; plus, I don't mind admitting I got lucky. I'll apologise for that too if you want.' Sandi's skin burned. 'My folks had almost nothing when I was growing up. My father lost his job in the mines, and he's never been able to get anything full-time again. He did any odd jobs to bring in money to feed us, and so did my mom.' He ploughed on, his voice harsh and uncompromising. 'The only break they got was when my career took off and I could finally help them out.'

'I'm sure they were grateful.' Sandi stumbled over her words. 'Look, I'd better be going.'

'Yeah, I think you better had,' he muttered and turned away, resting his elbows on the sea wall and staring out over the horizon.

Sandi scurried away, and when she checked back over her shoulder, Kieran ' hadn't moved. She'd spoiled everything over a silly ice cream; but maybe, in the long run, she'd done them both a favour.

18

Kieran made up his mind, and instantly a weight lifted from his shoulders. Before he could have any second thoughts, he texted Helen to turn down her offer to work together once and for all. Next, he sent a message to Nick, and told his manager he'd be in touch when he returned to Nashville, and not to contact him until then. He turned off his phone before he could get any irate replies. When he got back to the house, he put a cheque for Sandi in an envelope, along with a note saying he didn't need a housekeeper any longer.

He was done pretending with all of them. Kieran knew he should get in touch with his mother, but hopefully he'd get a few weeks' grace before she started to bug him. Dropping out of sight for a few days might not be a bad idea.

'What do you think, Peter?' He'd got

into the slightly nutty habit of talking aloud to his dead relative. 'Have I finally got some guts?' Sandi's assumptions about him based on a few dumb media stories had pushed him over the edge. She hadn't had the courage to ask him outright for an explanation, and had picked up a slew of garbled half-truths instead. He ran upstairs and threw a few things into his old backpack while he carried on the one-sided conversation. 'Fiddle or guitar? Guitar.' He took Peter's silence as agreement. He planned to hop into the car and head for St. Mawes, where he'd find somewhere to stay for a couple of nights and do some exploring. Luckily, he'd packed his hiking boots, and there were all kinds of neat coastal paths where he could work off the excess energy burning him up from the inside.

As he prepared to lock the front door, the hall phone started to ring. It wasn't a hard decision to ignore it, and he left without a backward glance. On the way out of Penarth, he popped Sandi's letter through her letterbox with only a brief pang of regret. A couple of hours later, Kieran was feeling better than he'd done in months.

He kicked off his shoes and stretched out on the narrow single bed to let his feet hang off the end. The tiny bed-and-breakfast he'd discovered while wandering the streets of St. Mawes was perfect for his escape plan. Mrs. Hawken fitted the picture he'd constructed of a housekeeper when he'd been looking to employ someone — before smart, clever Sandi turned up on his doorstep. Elsie Hawken was a short, dumpy woman with the sweetest smile, and she'd welcomed him with open arms. She'd chided him for being too thin, and spoken wistfully about Walt, the young American soldier who'd given Elsie her first kiss. Kieran heard the poignant story of his landlady's brief flirtation with one of the soldiers practising in Cornwall for the D-Day invasion.

My daughter found out on that internet thing that poor Walt died a few weeks after I met him. There was some

*tragedy up in Devon, at Slapton Sands,
when the Germans caught them out. It
were kept a secret for too long, but now
there's a memorial and everything. She's
taking me up to see it soon.*

The story instantly triggered a song
in his head, complete with a title—
'Sleeping Tiger', after the codename
of the disastrous Exercise Tiger that
had cost nearly eight hundred lives. He
strummed his guitar quietly, and tried not
to disturb his hostess who was downstairs
watching TV. The guitar wasn't his usual
instrument of choice but he'd brought
it with him to change things up. He'd
gravitated to the fiddle as a teenager after
being drawn to traditional West Virginia
roots music. Fans often commented on
the authenticity of his music, but he'd
never admitted that was because he'd
initially taught himself to play because
there was no money for lessons. It made
his music closer to the sound of old-time
musicians who'd done the same out of a
similar necessity.

Kieran rubbed at the sore spots on

his neck. He glanced at his watch and couldn't believe it was seven o'clock. No wonder his stomach was growling. He hadn't been this immersed in his music for a long time, and was forced to admit that the recent sessions with Helen had got his creative juices flowing again.

If he'd cared about creating a good impression, he'd have showered and put on clean clothes, but his old t-shirt and shorts would do fine for what he had planned. All he had in mind was to find a decent pub where he could eat a filling dinner and drink a few pints of good Cornish ale. He'd walk back to *Shangri-La* afterwards for a long sleep, unfettered by anyone else's opinions and expectations.

This was the best idea he'd had in forever.

* * *

'Where is he? I bet he's here!' Helen screeched. 'This is all your fault.'

Sandi quickly stepped out over her

140

front step and closed the door behind her.

'Don't give me that innocent look. You might've fooled Kee, but that's because he's naive where women are concerned,' Helen scoffed.

At a wild guess, Sandi guessed the woman had also received a message from Kieran. His letter had been on her mat when she'd arrived home with Pip, and she'd instantly recognized his distinctive scrawl. She'd shoved the envelope in her pocket and struggled to concentrate on Pip's enthusiastic description of his visit with Mike. He'd got on well with his father, and Keri had been a hit as well. She'd thoughtfully stayed behind while his father took him out to lunch, and later produced a book about the Knights of the Round Table, happily reading it with him multiple times.

When Sandi finally managed to glance through Kieran's brief note, it had taken all her resolve not to cry. If she didn't so badly need the money, she would have torn up his generous cheque — but money was money, and principles didn't pay bills.

'Could you please keep your voice down?' Sandi begged. Pip didn't need to hear them arguing, and neither did her neighbours.

'Tell me where he is and I'll leave.'

At least she had no need to lie. Sandi explained that Kieran hadn't told her either, and had only mentioned going away for a couple of days without giving any details.

'He was all set to work with me again,' Helen insisted. 'I'll bet you talked him out of it and changed his mind.'

Why she thought Sandi had any influence over Kieran was a mystery. From everything she'd read online, he'd be an idiot to trust Helen again — but that wasn't her business, no matter how much she might wish it were.

'I'm Kieran's housekeeper, nothing more. At least, I *was*.'

Helen's eyes narrowed. 'Did he sack you?'

Sacking implied incompetence, and

there'd been no such suggestion, but Sandi decided it'd be in her best interests to agree.

'I'll be staying at the White Hart until Mr. Kieran O'Neill reappears. He's not messing *me* around. He needs me.' She tossed her hair back over her shoulders. 'If you hear from him, call me. I'll pay you well.'

'How dare you,' Sandi snapped. 'Get out of my sight, and don't you dare come near me or my family again.' Helen's mouth gaped open, and Sandi hurried back inside while she could. Her hands shook as she struggled to lock the door.

'Mummy. Can we have ice cream now? You promised,' Pip pleaded. 'Where were you?'

He'd be disappointed about losing Kieran's friendship, but thank goodness she hadn't allowed anything further to develop between them. This was why she didn't do 'boyfriends'.

'Someone came to the door looking for directions.' She hated to tell a lie, but for once she took the easy way out. 'Come on. Ice cream time.' Any confusion he might have had about her whereabouts flew away as the question of how much ice cream he could talk her into filled Pip's head.

★ ★ ★

With Pip tucked up in a bed and a glass of wine in her hand, Sandi reread Kieran's letter. There was nothing personal in the few brief sentences, and that hurt the most. In its own way, the scarcity of words spoke volumes. He'd treated her as nothing more than a temporary employee, and in the process made his feelings perfectly clear.

Like most people, he could only take being rejected so many times. Ice cream. Tintagel. A cup of coffee. Simple things, really, but so much more had been layered under his offers. They'd both known it.

Sandi could understand him turning his back on her, but what had gone wrong with Helen? She'd got the impression that the music between them had gone well yesterday even if their personal relationship was a challenge. In terms of getting his reputation back it made sense to work with Helen — so what had sent him into reverse gear? The deal with Kieran clearly meant a lot to the other woman, and Sandi wasn't sure she'd give up easily.

A weary tiredness swept through her, and she knew she needed to stop this merry-go-round of confusing thoughts. Tomorrow would be another long, busy day, and if she didn't get a decent amount of sleep she'd hit the ground dragging in the morning. Hopefully Kieran wouldn't muscle in on her dreams again.

You want him there. Admit the truth for once.

Sometimes being honest hurt.

19

Kieran tapped his foot in time with the music, and sang along with the rest of the crowd of people crammed into the tiny pub. He'd asked Mrs Hawken for a recommendation, and she'd advised him to avoid the larger, more popular places along by the water and walk further along the road towards St. Mawes castle. The Treffry Inn, named after the castle's sixteenth-century builder, wouldn't have been any good for cat-swinging; in fact, even a baby mouse would have proven a challenge.

Remember to duck your head when you go in, my 'andsome. They weren't big men in those days, and they wood beams will get you if you'm not careful.

So far, Kieran had avoided bodily injury. He'd found an empty table tucked in the back corner of the room, and ordered a plate of fish and chips. He'd been surprised when a group of three musicians appeared carrying a fiddle and guitars. Soon the place had filled with the sounds of a traditional Cornish folk song and everyone started to join in.

'There you go.' A smiling teenage girl set an overflowing plate of food in front of him and a small wooden crate full of different condiments. 'You'll want the salt and vinegar.' He guessed that was code for *I know you're a foreigner, and that's how they're eaten.*

There was no danger of him going hungry tonight, because a family of four would have been perfectly content with the amount of food he'd received. He'd heard British portions were on the small side, but obviously the Treffry Inn hadn't got that message. Somehow he finished it all and made his way back up to the bar for another pint of beer.

'The Fal River Boys are good, aren't they?' the landlord asked, gesturing towards the group who were getting ready to play again. 'I shouldn't tell you to check out the competition, but if you're still around tomorrow night, the 'Smugglers' Secrets' group are doing a gig at the Warleggan Arms. They're at the top of the heap in the Cornish folk scene, and it's a rare chance to hear them. The place will be packed.'

A curl of excitement unfurled in Kieran's gut. Discovering new music always thrilled him, and tonight had rekindled his interest. A brief picture of Sandi's smiling face snaked its way into his thoughts. If only she was with him now, they could've eaten together and enjoyed sharing the music … Kieran stopped the treacherous ideas there. He didn't need to think about anything connected to her. Not his aching need to be with her. And definitely not how she must've felt on reading his brief, impersonal message.

'Another pint of Trelawny?'

He realised the landlord was speaking and managed to nod his agreement. Kieran didn't bother going back to his table, and leaned on the bar instead, drinking deeply of the locally made pale

ale he'd fallen for in a big way. He was soon laughing as he listened intently to the lyrics of 'Lamorna'—an old tune about a man who meets up with a woman one night, only to discover that she's his own wife at the end of the evening.

'This'll be their last song. Always end with 'Trelawny', they do.' The landlord's pride was evident and it didn't take much to pry out of him the story of the seventeenth-century Cornish bishop who'd stood up to the King and lived to become a folk hero.

Before he knew it, Kieran was singing as loud as any Cornishman; and after the song finished, the landlord smiled broadly and slapped him on the shoulder.

'You've got some voice on you, mate. If you stay here long, they'll rope you into joining them.' He chuckled.

Kieran couldn't help thinking it wouldn't be a bad life as he made a non-committal response and said his good-byes. Outside the pub, the cool night air hit him full-on, and his longing for Sandi intensified. He dragged his phone out of his pocket and turned it on. Ignoring the myriad of texts that'd come in from Helen, he entered the number he knew by heart and held his breath.

★   ★   ★

Sandi answered the phone before it could wake up Pip. Far too late, she saw Kieran's number on the screen.

'Don't hang up, honey.'

'Do you know what time it is?'

'Time for me to talk to you?' he teased.

'Some of us were in bed asleep.' That wasn't the complete truth. The in-bed part was genuine, but her claim to have been asleep was wishful thinking. She'd already been staring at the ceiling for at least an hour.

'I need to apologise.'

'What for?'

'Heck, I don't know, a whole ton of stuff. Writing that rude letter. Pestering you when you're plainly not interested in me. I guess, mainly for being a stubborn American who doesn't know when he's beat.'

The breath left her body. *Not interested in him? He must be crazy.*

'Are you still there, Sandi? Don't hang up on me,' Kieran begged. 'I wish you were here. I could see your face and know better what you're thinking.'

Sandi could only be grateful for small mercies. Being at the other end of the phone was far safer. 'It's late. Go to bed.'

'I've been singing your national anthem.'

'Why on earth were you singing 'God Save the Queen'?'

Kieran's warm laughter filled the line. 'No, silly girl, the Cornish one. The landlord told me y'all considered 'Trelawny' to be your anthem.'

'Where in heaven's name are you?'

'St. Mawes.'

Against her will, she found herself asking how he'd ended up there, and listened to his convoluted story about a folk group he wanted to hear tomorrow, and what had made him go today instead. She ignored the dig about her turning

151

cold on him, and focused on what he had to say about Helen Ross. He explained the whole legal mess with his ex-partner.

'I can't trust her.'

'No, I don't think you can.' Sandi considered mentioning Helen's visit earlier in the evening, but held her tongue.

'Come to me, Sandi.' Before she could ask if he seriously thought she was going to make her way to St. Mawes at nearly midnight, Kieran laughed. 'I've done it again, haven't I? We seem to spend half our time at cross-purposes. I meant tomorrow. Ask your folks to look after Pip for the evening, so you can come and have dinner with me and listen to 'Smugglers' Secrets'. I'll drive back to Penarth and pick you up, then bring you home again afterwards. It's an evening out. Nothing more.'

Could it really be 'nothing more'? She doubted it — but Sandi hadn't wanted to say yes to anything this badly for a very long time.

'Think about it and call me in the morning.'

'You might have changed your mind,' she half-whispered.

'Honey, I'm not gonna do that. Not after it took all the courage I've got to phone you in the first place.' Kieran sighed. 'You can be a tad intimidating, and I'm an all-out wimp when it comes to asking women out on dates.'

She took a couple of steadying breaths before replying. 'Is that what this is?'

'Yeah, I guess so. Have I blown my chances now?'

The idea of the handsome, funny, talented Kieran being so uncertain gave her courage. 'No ... but I'm not making a rash decision, because it's not my way.' Sometimes she wished she were different and could throw caution to the wind, but that wasn't her nature. 'Don't get me wrong, I'm not trying to make too much of this ... but I haven't been on a date since my marriage failed.' Sandi stopped herself there. 'I'm going back to sleep, and you ought to get back to your B&B before your landlady sends out a search party. We'll talk tomorrow.' She hung up before he thought of something else to keep her there any longer. Sandi was very afraid Kieran could talk her into things she shouldn't say yes to.

20

'Why can't I go too?' Pip protested. 'Mr. O'Neill likes me. He said all redheads have to stick together.' His lower lip wobbled along with Sandi's resolve.

'You'd be bored,' his grandmother intervened. 'They're going to listen to grown-up music. We'll have much more fun. Anyway, it's the same as you going out to play with your friends. You don't always want Mummy there.'

Terrible analogy, Mum.

'But Mr. O'Neill's *my* friend.'

Sandi crouched down and grasped Pip's hands. 'I know he is, but ... he's mine too.' A hot rush of embarrassment flooded her cheeks. She wished she'd never mentioned Kieran's offer to her mother over the phone, because in one instant the whole thing had snowballed. Jean had ordered her to bring Pip over right away, and when they arrived, her mother steamrollered every one of Sandi's objections. She'd been backed up by her husband, who'd plainly been primed beforehand. 'You always like getting the chance to sleep over with Nana and Grandpa.'

Pip frowned. 'When are you coming back?'

'Past your bedtime. Mummy won't want to wake you and bring you home then. I'll take you to school in the morning,' Sandi's mother said firmly, putting a stop to her daughter's attempt to give him a more detailed explanation. 'Why don't you both stay for lunch? I've got a big joint of beef.' Jean smiled at Pip. 'If someone is a good boy, he might get to help Grandpa make the Yorkshire puddings.' Sandi forced herself not to say how much mess that would make, remembering how much Pip had enjoyed cooking with Kieran the other day.

'Yippee!' Pip beamed. His reservations about her evening out were seemingly forgotten. Everyone appeared to have made up Sandi's mind for her, which meant she had no excuse to put off ringing Kieran any longer.

'I'm going to, um … ' She waved her phone around and hurried outside before she received more unwanted advice. Kieran answered immediately, and she rushed to accept his invitation before she lost her nerve. 'If you've changed your mind, I'll understand.'

'You don't get out of it that easy.' Kieran chuckled. 'You've said yes. There's no going back on your word now.'

'I don't go … '

'Relax. I'm teasing.'

She was out of practise with this — if she'd ever been in it to start with. Mike had been her first serious boyfriend, and a good sense of humour wasn't one of his strengths. From the distance of time, Sandi saw that as a huge black mark. All of the happily married solid couples she knew, including her parents, found something to laugh about together even in the darkest times.

'I know. I don't mean to be so … ' She struggled for the right word

— considering *prissy*, *boring* and *strait-laced* before rejecting them out of hand. '... serious all the time.'

'I know, honey.' Kieran's quiet response eased a few of the worries she couldn't seem to let go of. 'Is four o'clock this afternoon too soon for me to come pick you up? It's a beautiful day, and I thought we could take a walk around St. Mawes before eating an early dinner. I've booked us a table at the Warleggan Arms. The food's supposed to be good, and it'll guarantee us a seat for the concert.'

She couldn't believe he was going to all this trouble to spend a few hours with her.

'Don't overthink this. Remember what I said?'

It's an evening out. Nothing more. The words were etched in her brain.

'Yeah. Thought you would.' His warm laughter trickled down the phone. 'You want me to collect you from your folks' place? I assume young Pip will be staying with them.'

Sandi's throat tightened. She appreciated his thoughtfulness more than she could express. Despite the fact she was a grown woman with a child, Kieran wanted to do things the right way.

'That's kind, but I'll be going back to my flat to get ready, so you can come there to pick me up. Apart from anything, Pip would pounce on you and we'd never get away.' She didn't mention her son's initial reservations about them going out. Sandi was always a long-term planner, and had been awake half the night going through different scenarios — none of which ended well.

'He's a neat kid,' Kieran said. 'I'm really looking forward to seeing you later.' His gruff tone touched Sandi.

'Me too.' She kept it simple but honest, something they hadn't always been together. Saying goodbye seemed the best move before she could be tempted to add anything more.

★ ★ ★

If he didn't spend the rest of the day doing something energetic, Kieran knew he'd go crazy. After he picked his landlady's brains and scoured the guidebooks she had available for her guests, he settled on doing a tour of the castle before walking further along the coast. His plan was to return to St. Mawes no later than three o'clock, which should give him time to shower and change before driving the half-hour or so back to Penarth.

Cornwall had a grip on him already, but tightened its hold by ramping up its wild beauty with perfect walking weather, a sky so blue it dazzled, and views that even a top-notch writer couldn't hope to do justice to. He'd had a lifetime fascination with castles — maybe the lack of them in West Virginia had stoked his imagination — so he wasn't about to miss out on the chance to check one out close-up. The view across the Fal estuary to another castle at Pendennis was spectacular, and the guide explained that both castles had been built by King Henry VIII as part of his coastal defences. Kieran couldn't help painting musical pictures in his head of the people who'd lived and worked there in medieval times, and none of it resembled anything he'd created before.

After taking a ton of photos, he left the castle and followed the coastal path along by the River Fal. Mrs. Hawken had recommended walking the three miles or so to the small village of St. Just in Roseland. She'd told him Sir John Betjeman, one of England's greatest poets, had described the church there as 'the most beautiful on earth', and Kieran wanted to see it for himself.

The fascinating thirteenth century-church built on the site of an original sixth-century Celtic chapel inspired him too, and he composed a soundtrack in his head as he walked around. He kept having to take out his phone to record snippets of music and lyrics before they disappeared. He strolled around the sub-tropical gardens down by the water, and took time to wander around the ancient graveyard.

161

Despite Mrs. Hawken's mammoth breakfast, Kieran was starving again. He wasn't in the mood for company, and ignored the couple of popular pubs to buy a large hot pasty from the village shop instead. He took it down by the water to eat, and Sandi drifted back into his mind as she so often did. If he messed up tonight he might blow the only chance he'd get with her.

It suddenly occurred to him that he'd brought nothing respectable to wear, and he rejected the idea of going back to *Gwel an Mor* to change. If he didn't linger on the walk back, he'd have time to scour the few shops in St. Mawes — although the selection would probably be limited to sailing gear or souvenir t-shirts. Sandi deserved for him to at least make an effort.

He screwed up the paper bag containing his pasty crumbs and tossed it in the trash. Operation Win Over Sandi was about to commence.

★　★　★

Everything she owned was wrong. Too severe or too fussy. Too dark or too light. The clock ticked relentlessly and Sandi's anxiety grew along with the pile of rejected clothes strewn over the bed. When her mother had packed her off home after lunch to have plenty of time to get ready, she'd almost pleaded to be allowed to stay. Playing Go Fish with Pip struck her as infinitely more appealing than getting ready for a date she was rapidly losing the nerve for.

It's Kieran. You like him. He's easygoing, charming, and fun to be around. That logic fought against the crazy, emotional rant filling her head. *He's too handsome, too rich, and too everything for the likes of you.* For two pins she'd ring and cancel, but her innate good manners wouldn't let her do that to him. It was too late anyway, because he'd be knocking on her door in less than ten minutes.

It's an evening out. Nothing more. She repeated the mantra until the tension holding her body in a tight knot eased slightly. Before she could change her mind again, Sandi tugged back on the sleeveless turquoise linen dress she'd started out wearing. Worn with simple silver jewellery, white wedge sandals and a soft pashmina in case she got cold later, she decided she looked decent enough and stopped fussing.

She couldn't remember the last time she'd worn perfume, but dabbed a little on now for courage. The shrill ring of the doorbell echoed through the quiet flat and Sandi's heart raced.

Forcing herself to stand still for a few seconds, she checked her appearance one last time in the mirror before walking as slowly as she could manage out through the bedroom and into the hall.

Sandi unhitched the security chain and opened the door.

'Oh.' Her prospects of a good evening fizzled.

21

Kieran chewed on a breath mint, smoothed down his hair, and got out of the car. He was a couple of minutes early, but hoped Sandi wouldn't mind. Outside the door, his finger hovered over the bell for a second before he gave it two short jabs.

'Come in.' Sandi instantly opened the door and frowned at him.

'What's wrong? Is it Pip?'

'No. You've got a visitor.' Without giving him a chance to ask any questions, Sandi walked away from him, giving Kieran no choice but to follow.

'The wanderer returns.' Helen unfurled her long legs and got up from the sofa. 'Ms. Thomas tried to tell me she didn't know where you were, but I knew she was lying.'

Kieran's head spun. 'I thought you'd have left Cornwall by now.'

Helen's laughter ricocheted around the room. 'You mean you hoped I had.'

'Ms. Ross has been following me.' Sandi's distaste ran through her taut, clipped words. 'And listening at open windows.'

'It's not my fault you were boasting to your mother about your date.' She pointed a long red fingernail in Kieran's direction.

'You had no right to be lurking outside in the first place.'

'The last I heard, England's a free country,' Helen retorted.

If he didn't step in, there would be all-out war in a minute. 'Hey, take it easy, ladies. Let's all sit down.'

'I want her out of my house. Now.' Sandi clicked her fingers.

'Helen. We're going to find somewhere for a quick chat.' If he could manage to placate her, there was still a chance of salvaging his evening with Sandi. Kieran made a grab for his ex-girlfriend's hand. 'Sandi. I'll be back in fifteen minutes, and we'll go out as planned.' Both women tried to speak, but he ignored them and walked out, pulling Helen along in his wake.

'Let me go,' she hissed.

'Nope.' Kieran led her down towards the harbour and pointed towards the café. 'We're going in here. And behave. I don't want to cause a ruckus.' She shrugged and followed him in. Mel's eyebrows rose when she spotted him, and shot up to the ceiling when he led Helen towards his favourite table by the window. 'Two coffees, please, Mel.'

'Quite at home, aren't you?' Helen sniped.

'Yeah. I like it here. Got a problem with that?'

She didn't answer until they got their drinks.

'Actually, I do. A big problem.' Helen rested her elbows on the table and focused hard on him. 'What went wrong, Kee? One minute we're making great music together again, and the next you send me a stupid text and disappear.'

He leaned back in the chair. 'You

caught me unawares and I needed to think a few things through.' A wave of utter certainty washed over him. 'I want a different life. I'm not sure of the details yet, but I'm getting there.'

Helen scoffed. 'Is this because of your little English rose?'

Kieran didn't intend to deny Sandi's part in his plans, but he'd no right to make her the centre — at least, not yet. Keeping his voice low, he tried to explain the way being at *Gwel an Mor* made him feel, and the new ways he was exploring his music. A brief hint of softness blurred the edges of Helen's sullen expression.

'That's all very well, but where does that leave me?' She glowered. 'You'll get tired of playing Happy Families. I know you too well.'

You really don't.

'You live for your music, and it's never better than when we're working together. Admit it.' Her face tightened. 'I really need a hit, Kee.'

After all she'd done, Helen still expected him to come through for her. Kieran couldn't believe what he was hearing.

'I know I behaved badly, and I'm sorry.' Helen fiddled with her napkin. 'I was under a lot of pressure.'

'Who from?'

'I can't tell you.'

'Then there's no way I can help.'

'Fine.' She exhaled a heavy sigh. 'My dad's a bit of a gambler.' Helen's eyes swam with tears and she wiped them away with her hand. 'No. That's a lie. He's addicted to gambling. We were about to lose our family home and my mom begged me for help.'

The knowledge that there had been more to Helen's betrayal than simple greed somehow helped. 'We were supposed to be in love, but you didn't share all this with me or ask for my help. I don't get that.'

Her hands shook as she tried to take a sip of coffee, and she gave up, setting the cup back down on the table. 'Prometheus Records offered to sign me, but I lacked the songwriting credentials they were looking for. In a moment of madness, I embroidered how much I'd helped you with 'The Lonely Miner'.'

"Embroidered'? You flat-out lied about writing it yourself! You didn't come in on it until I asked you for help with the harmonies. I credited you with that, and you'd have got your share of the earnings.'

'It wouldn't have been enough. I did what I had to for my family. I'm real sorry you got hurt in the process.'

'And that's supposed to make me feel better?'

'Not really.' She sighed. 'I'm planning to confess everything, and you'll be completely exonerated. I need to do this for my own sake, whatever you decide.'

There was another question he needed to ask, although it was hard to force the words out. 'While you're on an honesty kick, tell me this — did you ever love me? And I mean *me*, not Kieran O'Neill, songwriter.'

'In a way.'

She couldn't meet his eyes, and her evasive answer told him everything he needed to know. Kieran's brief pang of regret for their shared past drifted away and a sense of freedom surged through him. 'I've gotta go. Take care of yourself, okay.'

Helen's eyes flared. 'That's it?'

'Yeah. That's it. I appreciate what you're going to do to put things right, and I hope your father gets some help, but there's no way I can work with you again. There'd be no trust between us — at least not on my side.' Without another word, he stood up and walked over to Mel to pay for the coffee. He guessed she'd listened to as much of his conversation as she could manage. It didn't matter, though — because he planned on telling Sandi everything tonight.

★ ★ ★

This wasn't how she'd imagined the evening going. Stilted conversation. No jokes. And Kieran fixing his gaze on the road ahead of them as if a herd of elephants might appear at any minute to trample the car.

'It's a beautiful evening.' She made another attempt to break the awkward silence.

'It sure is.'

This was partly her own fault. She'd overreacted to Helen's appearance, but it had been such a shock, and she wished he could be more understanding. Out of the blue, Kieran pulled the car over and stopped in a lay-by.

'I'm sorry, honey. I've spoilt our date before it even starts.' He grimaced.

'Only if you want it to be spoilt. I don't get out much. I've been really looking forward to this.' Sandi decided that wasn't the most tactful phrasing. She didn't want him to think she supposed any date was better than none, and tumbled over her words trying to explain herself.

A broad smile creased his face. 'Oh, Sandi, I'm not laughing at you. But you're a darned funny woman, even when you don't mean to be.' His emerald eyes sparkled. 'How about we start all over again?'

The serious edge to his voice touched

her deep inside. She leaned over and kissed his cheek, and a hint of woodsy cologne drifted up from his warm skin.

'Good idea. Let's head on to St. Mawes and we can talk there.'

He nodded and trailed a finger down her cheek, lingering on the racing pulse in her neck. 'Talk. Yeah. Good idea.' Kieran shifted back in the seat and started to hum under his breath. She recognised the beginning of 'Trelawny' and couldn't help laughing.

'Concentrate on the road!'

'Yes, ma'am.' Kieran's amusement shone through and she laughed with him. This was how she'd expected they'd be together. Helen wasn't going to win after all.

Before she realised it, they were entering St. Mawes, and Kieran turned up a narrow side street.

'I reckoned I'd park here and we can walk down. If I don't bring you in to meet Mrs. Hawken, she'll never forgive me.' Quickly opening the door, he jumped out and ran around to her side. 'She's spotted us.' He waved towards the woman peering out of a window at them. 'Make sure to tell her you like my shirt.'

'Why?' That sounded blunt, and she hastened to cover up her rudeness. 'Not that there's anything wrong with it.' Kieran's nautical blue-and-white striped shirt paired with crisp navy chinos had rather taken her by surprise earlier, because it was nothing like his usual attire.

'I'll give you the full story later,' he whispered, 'just trust me for now.'

I do. Don't ask me why. But I do.

Kieran squeezed her hand. 'Thanks.'

'There you are, my 'andsome.' A stooped, grey-haired woman appeared at the door, wearing an old-fashioned floral apron over her dress. She beamed indulgently at Kieran and Sandi fought against giving in to a fit of giggles. Mrs. Hawken was clearly another willing victim of his effortless charm. 'This must be your young lady.' Sandi was scrutinised from head to toe and received a nod of approval. 'You'd better get on and have your dinner. Do you have your key?' She spoke as if Kieran was a ten-year-old boy and she was his mother making sure he'd be able to get back into the house after school.

He patted his trouser pocket. 'Sure do. I'll be late.' Kieran draped his arm around Sandi's shoulder and gave one of his heart-stopping smiles. 'I've got to take this lovely lady home first.'

'Have a good time.' Mrs. Hawken smiled. 'You'll enjoy some fine singing tonight.' She gestured towards Kieran. 'Make sure this one behaves himself. He's a cheeky man.'

The tips of his ears turned bright red and Sandi loved seeing him disconcerted. 'I'll try my best.' She remembered his request, and leaned closer to whisper in the landlady's ear: 'You must have worked some sort of magic to smarten him up. I love the shirt.'

'He haven't got much of a clue. My Bert were the same,' she confided.

'We'd better be going, if you two have finished mocking me.'

Neither of them took any notice of

Kieran's attempt to sound aggrieved, and they took their time saying goodbye before Sandi allowed him to drag her away.

'You didn't have to take it quite that far,' he half-heartedly complained.

'Yes, I really did,' Sandi joked, and he swiftly pulled her into his arms, planting a gentle kiss on her mouth before letting go.

With his strong, warm hand holding hers, a gentle breeze blowing in off the sea and the soft evening sunshine bathing the town, they walked together down the hill. Sandi wished she could freeze the moment. For the first time in years she wasn't fretting, worrying and planning about what might or might not happen.

'Let it go,' Kieran murmured.

'What?'

He rubbed a finger over the spot between her eyebrows. 'Whatever put the tiny furrow there when you were so happy.'

No one had ever understood her this

way before. Thrilled or terrified? Sandi couldn't decide which it made her feel.

22

Saying the right thing now was crucial. Sandi didn't need him to turn too serious and initiate a conversation it was far too early for them to have.

'How about we vow to simply have a good time tonight?' He stuck out his hand and a tiny half-smile tugged at her lips.

'Perfect.'

So are you. Saying that aloud would definitely freak her out, even more so than his previous touch of mindreading.

'Let's go. Our table's booked for six o'clock.' He was pleased when he slipped his arm around her waist and she didn't make an objection. On the way down the hill, he rambled on about his visit to the castle and St. Just, but struck a brick wall when he tried to explain the effect it had had on him. 'Here. Listen to this.' Pulling out his phone, he played a few of the song ideas he'd recorded on his walk.

She didn't say a word, and her pace slowed while she gave it her complete concentration. Kieran loved that about her. Everything she did was so whole-hearted. Finally, she turned to him and smiled. 'That's incredible. I can imagine it performed as a kind of modern Celtic opera. Maybe at the Minack Theatre.' He got caught up in her excitement as she described the open-air theatre close to Land's End. Then, from out of nowhere, the shutters went down and he lost her.

'What's up?'

Sandi shook her head. 'Listen to me. Goodness knows why I'm talking all that nonsense. You're not exactly going to stay in Cornwall once you've got Peter's house sorted.'

'I'm a free agent. It's not written in stone that I have to live in Nashville the rest of my life.' A rush of heat coloured her neck, and Kieran hurried to elaborate while he had her at a brief loss for words. He went into more detail about the court case and the damage it had done to his reputation. 'I initially came here only because my mother asked me too.' His throat tightened and he struggled to get a grip on his emotions. The last thing he wanted was to elicit Sandi's sympathy.

'She recognised you needed to escape a bad situation, and gave you an easy way out to take without losing face.'

Kieran shrugged. 'I guess.'

'But America is your home, and it's where you made incredible music. You can't give all that up.'

'It's possible to make music outside of Nashville.' He wasn't sure if he was cross at her or with himself. *Yourself, stupid.* He'd managed to spoil their date for the second time. 'Look. Can we try again? I don't know about you, but I'm hungry.'

Sandi threw him a withering glance. 'Liar. You've managed to kill both our appetites.'

'You going in or not, mate?'

Kieran stared at the ruddy-faced stranger trying to get by. He hadn't even realised they'd reached the Warleggan

Arms. 'Yeah, we are, aren't we?'

★ ★ ★

An evening out and nothing more. It'd always been a crazy notion. She'd go through with it now, but there mustn't be any question of a second date. They both had enough complications in their lives without throwing the possibility of a romance into the mix. With a brief nod she walked past both men and pushed open the pub door.

'I'll check on our table.' Kieran headed towards the bar.

Despite her sadness, she couldn't help admiring the easy way he wended in between the tables and ducked to avoid hitting his head on the low rafters. His rich copper hair hung thickly around his face, gleaming under the lights, and when he glanced around to give her a tentative smile she couldn't help responding.

'Over here, honey.' He reappeared by her side and took hold of her arm to guide her towards a table over by the fireplace.

'There are menus here and the specials are on the chalkboard.'

Studying the food on offer took a few minutes and saved them having to talk properly. In the end, she chose her standard favourite of scampi and chips. When Kieran left to place their orders up at the bar, Sandi took the time to look around her. The pub was rapidly filling up and she guessed that by the time the band started to play it'd be standing room only.

'One white wine.' Kieran set her glass on the table and pulled out the chair next to her to sit down. 'Cheers.'

'Cheers.' She made an effort to play along. 'I love old pubs when all the life hasn't been modernised out of them.'

'Yeah, me too. We haven't got anything like this in … ' Kieran's voice trailed away. Anything connected with the physical distance between their lives had suddenly become taboo. 'Have you heard Smugglers' Secrets perform before?'

'Only on the radio.' She'd never been a woman to chatter mindlessly, but tonight she was desperate to draw the conversation away from anything too personal. She rattled on about the various types of music she enjoyed. When she'd dated Mike, they'd both been big fans of live music; but once they married and Pip was on the way, there hadn't been the time or the money. Sandi fell silent under Kieran's intense stare.

'Don't stop,' he pleaded and took hold of her hands, stroking his warm fingers over her skin. 'I want to know more about you.'

Sandi pulled away. She didn't need him seeing too much. 'I'm not that interesting.'

'Gotta disagree with you there, honey.'

Every time he knew how to silence her. She gratefully spotted the young waitress bringing their food over, but when the loaded plate was put in front of her, Sandi's stomach rebelled at the idea of eating.

'I didn't get a chance earlier to tell you how lovely you're looking tonight.' Kieran fixed her with his appreciative gaze. 'That blue sure is a pretty colour on you.' He lowered his voice. 'Don't give up on us so easily. You've never been a quitter before. Don't start now.'

'But ... '

He leaned in and pressed a soft kiss on her lips before easing away. 'Your shrimp are getting cold.' Kieran picked up his knife and fork. He sliced through his own grilled steak and popped in a mouthful. 'My appetite seems to have returned.'

Sandi was confused. He appeared to be ignoring everything they'd crossed swords about earlier. Picking up her knife and fork, she started to eat because it was safer than talking. Halfway through her meal, she caught him watching her. 'What?'

'Are we okay?'

That was a very good question, and she didn't have a proper answer. 'I don't know.'

'You going to at least give us a chance? Please.' Kieran's whispered plea touched her heart and she couldn't find the strength to turn him down. A sudden brilliant smile lit up his face.

'What're you grinning for? I haven't said a word.'

'You didn't need to. Your face said it for you.' He playfully wagged a finger at her. 'Don't bother denying it. Finish your shrimp, and if you're a good girl I'll buy you a sticky toffee pudding before the singing starts.'

Despite the fact she normally preferred fresh fruit and lighter desserts, Sandi had retained a childish love for the super-sweet pudding, and had mentioned it to Kieran one day. She tried to look unimpressed, but he only winked and went back to finishing his steak and chips.

★　★　★

He'd been afraid he'd messed up completely, and at the last second had decided to take a huge gamble. For a few scary seconds, he'd been certain Sandi would turn him down — but his decision to act as though nothing was wrong had paid off. This was a tiny light at the end of a long, dark tunnel … but it was better than flat-out hopelessness. He wasn't fooling himself. The small breakthrough was a beginning. Nothing more.

'Pudding and another glass of wine?'

'How can I refuse?' Sandi teased.

If he'd been a little more sure of how things were between them, Kieran would've joked right back at her, but he didn't want to push his luck. He left her and made his way through the crowd to place their order. Carrying the drinks back to their table without spilling them was a challenge, but he made it as the landlord announced that the evening's entertainment was about to start.

They had a good line of sight from their table, and Kieran's anticipation ramped up as a group of eight men came into view, all jockeying for position on the small stage. Ranging in age from as young as twenty-five up to one man who had to be at least seventy, the only instruments they carried were an accordion and a guitar.

A hush fell on the room, and next

thing the rich, multi-layered *a cappella* strains of 'Sloop John B' filled the air. Kieran glanced at Sandi and she met his smile as he wrapped his arm around her shoulder.

He gave himself up to enjoying the music.

23

Sandi tried to recall when she'd been this happy, outside of special moments with Pip or her family, but drew a blank. Along with everyone else, she tapped her feet and sang along with the old sea shanties and traditional folk songs. When the people around them became aware of Kieran's deep, rich voice, a tingle of undeserved pride ran through her.

'Do you mind if I go up and have a chat to them?' Kieran asked. The group were on a break and mingling with the crowd. 'Come with me.'

She was sure he was only asking out of politeness.

'If I didn't want you along, I wouldn't have asked. Stop second-guessing me.'

'Sorry.' Sandi grasped his outstretched hand. 'It's a bad habit of mine.'

'It's the whole control thing, isn't it?'

'It drives my parents crazy.'

Kieran leaned in and kissed her cheek. 'It's okay. I'm sure as heck not perfect, so I appreciate the fact you're not, either.'

'How disappointing. I thought I'd found the one flawless man.' Sandi's voice wobbled as she made the effort to joke along with him. 'Come on, or you won't get a chance before they start singing again.'

She stayed by his side as he made a beeline for the smooth-voiced tenor who'd played guitar on a couple of songs. The singer introduced himself as Walt Pembarth, and almost immediately the conversation went over her head as he and Kieran swapped technical musical talk.

'Hey, Tom, guess who I've found?' Walt called over to one of the other singers. 'Kieran O'Neill from Nashville. You know, he wrote 'The Ballad of Mary Lou' and 'Lonely Miner'.'

'You got seen off there, mate, over the miner song. That girl pulled a fast one,' Tom declared.

'What makes you say that?'

'I'm right, aren't I?'

'Well, yeah, but … '

'But nothing. 'Tis clear as day to anyone who knows your music.' He smiled. 'We'll buy you a pint first, and then you're singing with us. Don't argue.' Kieran's protest was drowned out as the rest of the group overheard and joined in.

'I think it's a marvellous idea,' Sandi interjected.

'You would,' he mumbled. 'I knew I should've stayed sitting down.'

'Don't be grumpy. Enjoy yourself. I'm going back to our table to watch.' Getting the opportunity to see the side of Kieran he'd largely kept hidden would be a bonus on this curious evening.

⋆   ⋆   ⋆

He hadn't been this nervous in years. The fact that most people here didn't have a clue who he was didn't lessen his anxiety. Kieran took a deep swallow of Tribute and set the glass back down on the bar.

Walt Pembarth's glowing introduction didn't help his stress level, and it reminded him why he'd abandoned singing in public to stick to songwriting. Glancing over the heads of the crowd, he caught Sandi's eye, and the instant warmth of her smile did the trick. He took several deep, steadying breaths, and stood near the microphone. They let him take the lead, and he launched straight into 'The Ballad of Mary Lou'. Soon people were joining in, and Kieran allowed himself to relax and enjoy the moment. When Saul Commons played the first chords of 'The Lonely Miner' on the accordion, Kieran's nerve briefly faltered. But, as his most popular hit got into stride and the crowd started to clap and sing along, he reclaimed his song. He'd been a fool to let Helen take this from him.

'Thanks, mate,' Saul said as they finished.

'No. Thank *you.*' They'd no idea what that'd done for him. 'I'll leave you to it now.'

'Come back up at the end.' Walt laughed around at the rest of the group. 'We've got to get our honorary Smuggler singing 'Trelawny'.'

Kieran chuckled. 'Sounds good to me. The Fal River Boys sang it over at the Treffry Inn last night, so I've had a practice run.'

It wasn't easy to make his way back through the crowd because he had to stop frequently and speak to people, but finally he reached Sandi. She jumped up and flung her arms around his neck before giving him an enthusiastic kiss. For several magical seconds he stared deep into her shining blue eyes, and the world around them disappeared.

'Uh, I think we'd better sit down.' Sandi glanced around nervously. Kieran wasn't going to apologise for something he didn't regret, and gave a wry shrug to the people staring at them. Before she could object, he pulled her down to sit on his lap.

'It'll free a chair up for someone else,' he declared.

'Aren't you the noble one?'

'That's me, honey. I should've been one of the Knights of the Round Table. Sir Kieran. Has a cool ring to it, don't you think?'

Sandi rolled her eyes.

'Give in. I'm not letting go of you now.' She went quiet and settled in his arms. 'We're gonna take the long way back to Penarth.'

'Is there one?'

'Sure to be. I'm lousy at map-reading when I want to be,' Kieran promised. 'We haven't had near enough time to talk, and tomorrow it'll be hopeless again.' She opened her mouth to protest, but he kept talking. 'Don't take it the wrong way. I know you've got responsibilities. We both do.'

'Let's enjoy the music,' she whispered. Kieran would never argue with a suggestion like that.

★　★　★

They sat on the beach in the moonlight and Sandi leaned back against Kieran. She relished the comfort of his strong arms wrapped around her and his steady warm breaths on the back of her neck. It was easier to talk without facing him. She told him the whole story of her abandoned art degree and the sad unravelling of her marriage.

'You need to paint again.' His plain statement left no room for argument, and for once she didn't try. 'It'll be good for Pip to see you pursue your dreams. It's setting a good example for him in a different way.' Kieran let the thought hang between them. 'I'm guessing, if you'd let him, Mike would help out more.'

Sandi turned around to face him. 'How can you possibly know that?'

Kieran brushed a loose strand of hair away from her face. 'Tell me some more about him.'

His simple request pulled the rug from under her feet. Could she finally trust Kieran enough to open up and tell him everything?

'I'm not trying to steer you into a corner.'

'Aren't you? If you're so big on us talking, why don't you tell me what you and Helen had to say to each other this afternoon?'

'Sure. I'd be happy to. But we aren't done talking about you by a long chalk.'

Yes, we are.

'She implied that she was under pressure from someone, and I finally got it out of her.' Kieran explained the whole sad story. 'Do you see now why I couldn't ever work with her again?'

'I certainly do. Trust is everything.'

'Tonight was very ... empowering for me.' Kieran's fingers played with her hair while he spoke of his deep love for music. 'I really want to get back to the root of why I fell in love with music in the first place.'

Sandi wished she had the courage to admit she felt the same way about her art, but stayed mum.

'It does us all good to shake things up

sometimes. Keeps us from staying in our own safe little rut.' Now he was talking about them both. 'I'm planning to stay a lot longer in Cornwall and explore the folk scene here. I've got a million and one song ideas already, and I'll never get them all down if I live to be as old as Methuselah.'

To know he wasn't jumping on a plane back to Nashville anytime soon relaxed something deep inside Sandi. The knot of tension she'd been carrying around since she first realised how much Kieran was starting to mean to her loosened its grip.

'I'm not gonna rush you, sweetheart,' he whispered. 'I'd better get you home.'

'Yes. You had.' Kieran wasn't the only one with feelings they weren't sure what to do with yet.

Reluctantly, they got up, and brushed the sand from each other before walking hand in hand back to the car. Sandi wasn't sure what tomorrow would bring, but she'd keep today tucked in her store of good memories. They might be the only thing keeping her company when Kieran moved on. Despite everything, she knew he would one day.

24

He couldn't put his finger on when it had happened, but sometime during the evening Sandi had made up her mind against the chance of a future which included him. Kieran had done all that she'd asked for — telling her everything she wanted to know — but he'd received little in return. He got on well with Pip. Her parents liked him. They were definitely attracted to each other. What was the problem?

Time! You idiot. Have you ever heard of dating a woman? Getting to know her?

He needed to be patient. Sleep surely wouldn't come tonight, so he might as well work on his music. He poured a small measure of whisky into one of his great-uncle's monogrammed glasses and took a sip of the smooth amber liquid. He ambled into the study and set down his drink before picking up the guitar.

Everything else went away apart from the songs he was creating, and Kieran lost himself.

A sudden jangling noise broke his concentration, and he glanced up at the ornate Chinese clock on the mantelpiece. Who on earth was calling at three in the morning? It had better not be Helen again. Kieran hurried into the hall and snatched up the phone.

'Yeah.'

'That's no way to talk to your mama.'

'Mom, do you know what time it is?'

'Of course. It's three o'clock in the afternoon. I suppose you're having tea and scones?' She laughed.

'It's three in the morning, Mom. We're six hours in front of you. Not behind.'

'Oops, I'm sorry. I did try to call yesterday and you weren't there. Anyway you're awake aren't you? You don't sound at all sleepy.'

'Well, yeah, I was working.' The confession slipped out before he could bite it back. Now he'd have to put up with being questioned about when he'd got back into music; what he was working on; etcetera, etcetera …

'I knew it.' The triumph in her voice was unmistakeable. 'Your mother knew best sending you to Cornwall, didn't she?' If she were a cockerel, she'd be crowing.

'You sure did,' he conceded. 'Anyway, why are you calling?'

'Aren't I allowed to check on my son?'

'Of course you are.' Kieran started to tell her all about the house and Cornwall, but skimmed over his renewed interest in music. He didn't mention Helen, and avoided saying a word about Sandi and Pip.

'I was all set to surprise you, but your daddy wouldn't let me.'

'Surprise me in what way?'

'I'm flying into London on Thursday.'

Great. This wasn't what he needed. 'How long are you planning to stay?'

'I'm thinking to visit with you for a week or so, and then take off to do some sightseeing.'

He tried to sound enthusiastic but it was a challenge. The first thing he'd have to do was ask Sandi to come back to work. His mother would expect to find a housekeeper as he'd promised, or Kieran would be in trouble.

'I'll meet you at Heathrow airport and we'll drive down. The train journey is a bit tedious.'

'No, thanks. I've heard all about the cute trains, and want to ride one for myself. You can still come up here and then we'll do it together.'

By the time he managed to get off the phone he'd given her run down on the weather, the food, and what Penarth was like. Basically, the village was a quirky English version of the small town in West Virginia where he'd grown up — the sort of place where money was tight and everyone knew your business.

Kieran yawned. He'd give sleep another try and worry about his mother later.

* * *

For the first time in forever, Sandi hadn't set her alarm, and now she stared in amazement at the clock. Nine a.m. Her mother had insisted Pip would be fine going straight to school from their house and she didn't have to be at the café until after lunch. That gave her the luxury of a few hours to herself. She considered the various options, including tackling the ironing, cleaning the flat, or doing some cooking to put in the freezer for busy days. *Are there any other kind?*

She hopped out of bed and went into the kitchen to put the kettle on, munching on a slice of toast while she stared out of the window. In theory, the tiny garden was shared by the four flats in her building, but no one else apart from she and Pip ever used it. Sandi opened the back door and padded out barefoot onto the warm grass. By scrounging cuttings from everyone she knew, and buying up straggly, end-of-season plants at the local garden centre, she'd gradually transformed the long, narrow space.

Out of the blue, a picture framed in her head, and a curl of excitement trickled through her. Sandi rushed back inside and rooted around in the back of her wardrobe to pull out her watercolour paints, a sketch pad and her brushes. Refusing to think too much about the significance of what she was doing, she placed everything on the bed while she searched for her old clothes from art college. The act of putting on her ancient paint-stained jeans and a Royal Academy summer exhibition t-shirt brought tears to her eyes.

You need to paint again.

Kieran's words resonated in her head and she mentally thanked him. She was impatient to get started and soon had everything set up in a quiet corner of the garden. The awkwardness of her first brushstroke knocked her off-kilter, but her hand gradually relaxed and she slipped back into the rhythm of transferring her mind's vision to the paper. At some point, Sandi stretched and shook out her neck muscles before going back to work on a tricky part, trying to capture the textured moss on the slant of the shed roof.

'Knock, knock. Anyone there?' Kieran's good-humoured voice broke her concentration and she startled as the door out to the street opened.

'What are you doing here?'

He strolled across the grass towards her. 'Nice place you've got here. I came to see if you were still alive. Agnes called to ask if I'd seen you because she was worried. I offered to come and check. You weren't answering your doorbell, and she'd mentioned the possibility of you being in the garden, so I walked back here.'

'Why would Agnes be worried?'

Kieran's mischievous grin made her stomach flip.

'Have you taken a look at the time recently?'

She checked her watch. 'Oh, my goodness. It can't be.' Sandi jumped up from the stone wall she'd been perched on while she worked, and almost lost her balance until Kieran put a steadying hand on her arm. 'I've got to go or I'll lose my job.'

'Cool it, honey. I told Agnes where we spent the evening, and that it was late when I dropped you off here.' He took a step closer and peered at her painting. 'Wow!' He let out a low whistle. 'You've been holding out on me. You're good.'

Sandi tried to explain that it'd been a long time and she was out of practise, but her excuses dried up under the power of his dazzling smile. In the end, she simply thanked him and stared down at her feet.

'I'd apologise for barging in on you, but I'm not going to. You'd have kept this a secret, wouldn't you?'

She ached to deny it but her natural honesty wouldn't allow her to lie.

'I'll leave you to get ready.' Hurt ran through his voice, but she still held back.

'Thanks for coming over.'

'No problem.' He headed for the gate and stopped with his hand on the latch. 'Oh, by the way, I'm hoping you'll come back to work for me. My mother's flying in on Thursday, and she'll expect to see a housekeeper at *Gwel an Mor* or I'll be in trouble.'

'I wouldn't want that.' Sandi managed a faint smile. 'I can come tomorrow if you like?'

'Great. I won't be back until late morning because I'm seeing a book dealer in Falmouth.'

Before she could think of anything to say to make up for her reticence, Kieran left. She gathered up her paints and headed indoors. The sun had gone in.

25

Kieran stared at the bookseller in disbelief. 'You're kidding me?'

'No, sir, I wouldn't do that,' Mr. Rescorla assured him. 'I need to do some more checking, but I'm almost certain this is one of only three known first editions.'

After Sandi had returned the King Arthur book Pip found when he was visiting, Kieran had read it himself, become curious about the author, and done some checking up online. What he discovered had intrigued him, and now it seemed he might be right.

'One copy sold last year for over two million pounds at Sotheby's.' Mr. Rescorla gave a satisfied smile. 'It wasn't in as good a condition as yours, either.'

And Great-Uncle Peter lived without decent plumbing and existed on cut-price baked beans. Crazy.

'Do you want me to contact an expert I know in London, and put things in motion if he agrees with my valuation?'

'Not for the minute. The book belongs to my mother, so it will be up to her. She's arriving at the end of the week.' Kieran hastened to reassure the man he'd bring the book back if they made the decision to follow through. With a lot more care than he'd done on the way there, he placed the book back in the box he'd found to protect it.

'My recommendation would be to put it into your bank for safekeeping, sir.'

'I will do.' The idea of keeping such a potentially valuable item lying around the house terrified him. 'Thanks for your help.'

Kieran left the shop and strolled down by the harbour, giving the Maritime Museum a longing glance. It wasn't a smart idea to consider doing any sightseeing today. He'd head back home and work out his next move.

When he parked outside *Gwel an Mor*, he was surprised to see the front door open, but then he spotted Sandi washing down the black paint. Kieran's first instinct was to rush over and tell her about the bookseller's discovery, but he made himself hold back. He needed to find a way to share the money with Pip because if the kid hadn't found the book it could've ended up being sent to the charity shop by mistake. Kieran would have to be clever, because Sandi wouldn't accept the money without a fight.

'Nice morning,' he called out, and she stopped working to look at him with a tentative smile. If only he could recreate that magical sliver of time on Sunday when all had been right between them.

'It is. Did you have a good time in Falmouth?'

'Yeah. It's a neat place. A few of Peter's books are worth selling, if that's what my mother chooses to do.' He'd leave it at that for now. 'Have you been getting the house shipshape again?'

'I've only been gone a couple of days. Even *you* haven't had the chance to create too much chaos.' Sandi laughed, and he was almost dumb enough to say how good it was to see her smiling more. 'I'll finish washing down the door, then come in to get lunch ready. I wasn't sure what time you'd be back, so I've made cold poached salmon and potato salad, and I'll roast some asparagus to go with it.'

'You'll join me.' He didn't phrase it as a question, and after giving him a quiet stare she nodded. 'Fix it early so you can get down to the café on time. We can't have you being late again.' He took advantage of the fact that her hands were full with a scrubbing brush and a bucket of soapy water to pop a quick kiss on her cheek. As he hurried away, a sopping wet sponge caught him on the back of the neck.

'That'll teach you to hassle your employee.'

Kieran looked around at the mess he'd made. 'I'll clean up the floor.'

'Please don't. You'll make it worse. Go away and do something useful.'

'Like what?'

'Write another hit song.'

'How about a kiss first?'

Sandi tried to look stern, but the effect was spoiled by her sparkling eyes. 'Behave yourself. Maybe after lunch. That is, if you're a good boy and eat all your vegetables.'

'Yes, ma'am. Are we having squash?'

She shook her head. 'We're not eating *or* drinking that today. Now, get on with you.' With a broad smile, she shooed him away, and this time he obeyed. Spoiling magical moments between them wasn't going to happen again if he could help it.

*   *   *

Sandi was in trouble. She'd enjoyed her lunch with Kieran far too much, he was such good company, and she hadn't wanted to leave. It'd be far too easy to get used to him brightening her life. She strode down the hill away from *Gwel an Mor* and tried not to be distracted by the glittering powder-blue sea. One day, she'd make an attempt to capture the view, but right now she needed to hurry up.

Yesterday, Agnes and Mel had teased her unmercifully, and nothing she said would convince them she wasn't crazy over Kieran. If she was late for work again today, her co-workers would see it as further proof, and enjoy every moment. She'd worked there for five years, and until the last few weeks had never given them any personal ammunition to use against her. Now they had so much, they weren't sure which to use first.

A man standing outside the Copper Kettle moved towards her as she approached.

'Mike! What are you doing here?'

'Trying to track you down. You've been ignoring all my texts and phone calls.'

'It's only been a few days. I'm busy.' She tried to imply he was being unreasonable while knowing deep down he really wasn't. When he'd dropped Pip off on Saturday, he'd left a message with her mother that he wanted to make plans for another visit, but she'd ignored it.

Mike shifted from one foot to the other, not quite meeting her eyes for a few seconds before glancing back up. 'Look, I know I messed up when Pip was born.'

Understatement.

'I thought he had a good time with us on Saturday?' His bewildered uncertainty struck a chord with Sandi, and she couldn't bring herself to lie.

'He did.'

Mike's body-language spelled out his awkwardness, and she got the impression he was holding back on saying something.

'What is it?'

'Sandi, I don't want to stir up trouble.'

'But?'

'If you can't be reasonable about me and Keri seeing Pip regularly ... I'll have to see a solicitor and get a proper agreement.'

'Is this Keri's idea?'

An ugly red flush of heat coloured his

neck. 'Kind of.' He rushed on before she could interrupt: 'But she only put into words what I've been thinking.'

Sandi struggled to be honest. 'I don't want to be at odds with you.'

'Don't you?' He exhaled a heavy sigh. 'I know you've had a tough time. I don't expect you to forgive me, but for Pip's sake, can't we make an effort?'

'You mean, can't *I*?'

'I'm trying. Meet me halfway.' Mike pleaded.

'Give me a little time. Please.' Sandi tried to explain that she was trying to adjust to the idea of him being back in their lives. Protecting Pip from being hurt if his father disappeared again was her number-one priority. 'Can't you see my point of view?'

He nodded. 'Of course I can. I was young and foolish. I loved you — as far as any nineteen-year-old boy can love — but when Pip arrived, everything changed, and I wasn't prepared. I know you weren't, either, and there's no excuse. I really am sorry.'

Sandi touched his arm. 'It wasn't all your fault.' She took a deep breath. It was time to admit the truth. 'I was too young as well, and I'd never had a boyfriend. I got caught up in the excitement of getting married, but the reality of everyday life wasn't quite what I'd imagined.'

'Thanks. I appreciate you saying that. It's good to know it wasn't simply me.' His voice cracked. 'It was seeing Pip so tiny and helpless when he was born that scared me. All that responsibility … ' Mike shook his head.

'I know.' She held back on saying that she'd been frightened too, because they both knew that. It needed to be left in the past now. 'How about if you see Pip every other Saturday until you … '

'Prove myself?' Mike interjected. 'Fair enough. Maybe next time you can meet Keri.'

'Maybe.'

'Saturday week?'

Sandi agreed, and watched Mike walk away, her heart lighter than it had been for a very long time. Five hours of washing dishes, dealing with customers and cleaning more floors would keep her physically occupied, but her jumbled-up mind was another story. Up until a few weeks ago, she'd been content with her quiet, routine life with Pip — but now everything was changing, and she wasn't sure how that made her feel. Would she really want to go back if she could? Maybe when she could answer that question honestly she'd know the way forward.

26

He'd failed to get any sleep in the airport hotel, and now Kieran was guzzling down an oversized cup of coffee with two extra shots of espresso as though his life depended on it. The meeting space outside the Customs area was already filling up, despite the fact that it was barely seven in the morning.

'Woo-hoo! I'm here.' His mother's raucous yell cut through his jangled thoughts. She rushed towards him, and he noticed she'd had her greying curls freshly dyed for travelling in a vibrant shade of red — a wild approximation of her original colour. A porter dragging an overloaded trolley struggled to catch up with her, and the sight of it made Kieran cringe. He should have mentioned the lack of luggage space on English trains.

He struggled to keep his balance as she flung herself at him. Anyone would think they'd been parted for three years instead of three weeks. He extricated himself from a rib-squeezing hug and pointed to the bags. 'Did you leave *anything* at home?'

'How was I supposed to know what I might need?' He held back on saying that before her lottery win, she hadn't even owned a suitcase. 'I'm dying for a decent cup of coffee. Lead me to one right now if you value your life.'

'Sure thing. Our train to Reading station leaves in about thirty minutes. That one will take about an hour, and we'll pick up the main train down to Cornwall from there. We should arrive by mid-afternoon.' Kieran noticed her staring. 'Do I have a stain on my shirt, or spinach between my teeth?'

'No, but you sure are looking good.' She kissed him on the cheek. 'I'm glad to see my boy back.'

He was speechless. There were so many reasons why his life was better these days, but the crowded thoroughfare of an airport wasn't the place to talk about them.

'It's all right. I won't embarrass you here.' Her throaty laugh made him happy because he hadn't heard it in a long while. If money was supposed to bring people happiness, it hadn't done a very good job with his mother. 'Lead the way.'

It wasn't hard to avoid difficult questions for a while, but once they were settled on the Penzance train, Maura's natural chattiness returned.

'Who's the girl?'

'What girl?' he murmured, not quite looking at her.

'I know you're back doing your music, and I guess you like Uncle Peter's house from what you've said. But I'm pretty sure it's more than that, and I'm guessing it's a woman — or, should I say, I'm hoping it is?'

If he dared to mention Sandi in any personal context, he'd be in trouble. But if he *didn't*, then the first time his mother saw the two of them together, her shrewd brain would instantly make the connection, and he'd be in even greater trouble.

Kieran refused to let himself think too much, and blurted out everything.

'A down-to-earth sensible woman without her head in the clouds or any outlandish ideas. Exactly what you need.'

She'd hit the nail on the head. The problem would come in trying to convince Sandi. But he was ready to fight for what he wanted — his music, Great-Uncle Peter's house, and the incredible love that'd sneaked up on him for Sandi and young Pip.

'When do I get to check out your cute little English girl?'

Sandi would scoff at his mother's description and declare that she'd never been 'cute', was far too old to be considered a girl, and being Cornish born and bred wasn't truly English, either.

'Uh, tomorrow morning.'

'Good.'

Kieran started to talk about what he'd achieved so far with the house before remembering to ask how his father was doing.

'Okay, I guess.' Maura frowned. 'He wasn't too happy about me coming here.'

'Why not?'

'Lots of reasons. Don't you go fretting. We'll sort it out.'

His mother was jet-lagged and not thinking straight right now, but as soon as she recovered, things were going to have to change. They needed to get their family back on track.

'Listen to this. I've got a great story to tell you about one of Peter's books.' Swiftly, he launched into the tale of the famous King Arthur book, and couldn't help noticing his mother's obvious relief.

★ ★ ★

Sandi left the back door into her flat wide open so she'd hear Pip if he called for her in his sleep. Twilight was just setting in and casting interesting, elusive shadows over the garden. If Sandi was lucky, she'd be able to sneak in an hour of quiet painting before it became too dark. Over the last couple of days she hadn't been able to resist keeping on looking at the picture she'd started on Monday. She'd mentally added more layers to the story she was trying to tell. Kieran was right. If she really wanted to do this, she'd make the time. Watching inane TV programmes, cleaning house obsessively, and her insistence on ironing everything were all time-wasters. The freeing realisation made her smile.

The delicate fragrance of sweet lilac drifted across the garden, and Sandi took it as a sign to make capturing the beauty of the purple flowers her mission tonight. The plant's narrow window of flowering was transient, but right now it was in full bloom — rather like her opportunity to paint. Sandi loved the older-style flowers, and had rescued this particular plant from the local doctor's house when he'd been clearing out his garden.

A faint clicking sound disturbed her, and she glanced up to see Kieran standing by the gate. His tentative smile, as if he wasn't sure if he'd be welcomed, warmed her heart. She beckoned him over.

'I'm disturbing you,' he apologised.

'Tell me something new.' Sandi stood and reached up to wrap her arms around his neck. The combination of being with him again, the moonlight and the heady garden scents, made her senses reel.

'I missed you today,' Kieran whispered.

'I missed you too.' Until today, she hadn't realised how much his presence made *Gwel an Mor* a home instead of simply a house to clean. She'd missed the sound of him strumming on the guitar and his heavy footsteps as he came into the kitchen searching for her. 'Did your mum get here okay?'

'Yeah.' He stared deep into her eyes and rested his hand gently against her cheek. 'I told her about you.'

'I assume you don't mean simply the fact I'm your housekeeper?'

He shook his head. 'Correct first time, clever girl.'

'Oh.'

'She guessed.' An amused smile

creased his handsome face. 'It's what mothers do. You should know that.'

'I suppose I do.' She wasn't sure whether the information made her feel worried about the assumptions his mother might make or pleased that he considered their relationship important enough to share.

'I've got mixed feelings too, honey, but I couldn't lie to her. It was all my fault for looking too good, apparently.'

'That's always been your problem, in my personal view,' she sighed. If he were a peacock, he'd have preened his feathers and strutted around the garden; but instead he indulged in a smile that could only be described as smug. 'Don't be vain.'

'Sorry.' He didn't sound in the least apologetic. 'You want to sit down?'

'On your lap?'

Kieran grinned. 'I only see one chair, so there's no choice.'

'There's always a choice.' Her quiet, enigmatic words made his smile falter.

'I'm not talking about today, or even

tomorrow, but do you think I might ever be yours?'

'My what?'

'Choice.'

A seagull squawking on a nearby roof was the only sound outside of Sandi's racing heart.

'Maybe. But … '

'Shush.' Kieran pressed a soft kiss on her mouth. 'That's all I need for now. I wanted to make sure we were on the same page.'

'Mummy!' Pip's shrill voice rang out, and Sandi startled. 'I want another story. I'm not sleepy.'

'All right, I'll come in.'

Pip's curious gaze shifted to Kieran. 'Why was Mr. O'Neill kissing you?'

She struggled to come up with a satisfactory answer, but Kieran crouched down and rested his hands on Pip's shoulders.

'Adults often kiss when they like each other, and I like your mummy very much.' His simple reply touched her heart.

'Does she like you too?'

225

'Ask her yourself.' He glanced over Pip's shoulder and caught her eye. *Your turn.*

'Mummy?'

Sandi nodded. 'Yes, I do.'

'Good.' Pip grinned. 'Can I come to your house lots now, and cook and read all your books?'

'Whenever your mom says it's okay.'

Pip looked thoughtful. 'Are you going to marry my mummy and be my new daddy?'

'It's like this, Pip.' A surge of love swept through Sandi for this incredibly special man. He recognised that Pip was mature for his age, and needed to be given rational explanations for everything — from what stars were made of, up to why it was dangerous to play with matches. 'You already have a daddy who loves you very much. When me and your mom have known each other a bit longer, we might think about being a family together. If we do, I promise we'll ask you what you think of the idea first. Okay?'

Pip stuck out his hand. 'Shake.'

Sandi blinked away tears as her two special men shook hands.

Remember, a man's handshake is important. It's a promise he never breaks.

'Now, how about I read you a story while your mom gets her painting things put away? I bet you've got some King Arthur books I haven't seen.'

'I do. I do.' Pip jumped up and down. 'Come on.' He tugged on Kieran's hand.

'Sorry,' Kieran mouthed over Pip's shoulder.

She'd make sure later that he understood he had no need to apologise. For anything. Now Sandi knew she wouldn't turn the clock back, even if she could. Her life was pretty good right where it was.

27

'For heaven's sake, don't they have any decent showers in this country?'

Kieran struggled awake and sat up in the bed to see his mother standing in the doorway with a towel wrapped around her.

'We had better than your pitiful excuse for a bathtub growing up in the backwoods of West Virginia,' she declared with a snort. 'I've probably used all the hot water, so you'll have to make do with s quick wash before your girlfriend arrives.'

'Sandi isn't ... ' He'd almost denied the truth of his mother's definition, but it'd be a farce. 'Fine. I'm getting up in a minute.'

'Shoot.' His mother whistled and rushed across the room to stare out of his window. 'I was too tired for all that to register yesterday.'

Kieran felt as pleased as if he'd designed the view of Penarth for her pleasure. 'Cool, isn't it?'

'Yeah.' She glanced around at him. 'No wonder you don't want to leave.'

He didn't argue. They had a lot to talk about. 'Do you want a cup of coffee before I show you the whole house?'

'Does Sandi usually fix your breakfast?'

'She's always happy to if I'm hungry, but doesn't get here until after nine o'clock. If you're starving, I can cook you up something now.'

'I'll wait.' By the gleam in her eye, Kieran guessed she wasn't about to miss an opportunity to question Sandi. 'I'm going to get dressed. You can do the same. And wear something that doesn't make you look like something the cat dragged in.'

He hadn't realised she was *that* keen to get him married off.

'And don't answer me back.' Maura glared. 'Women always appreciate a man who makes an effort. She might say she doesn't care how you look, but trust me, she does.'

Kieran sighed. So much for his peaceful life. He'd stirred up a hornets' nest and was about to get stung. 'Fine.'

'Fifteen minutes. You'd better have a pot of strong coffee ready.' His mother swanned out of the room, and he fought the urge to bury his head under the covers and stay there.

★   ★   ★

Sandi let herself into the house when Kieran didn't answer the door, and heard voices upstairs so hurried on back to the kitchen. In the middle of the breakfast preparations, she heard footsteps in the hall and turned around with a smile, sure it was going to be her handsome employer.

'You must be the famous Sandi.'

She fixed her gaze on the tall, big-boned woman scrutinizing her as though Sandi were a interesting exhibit in a museum. Her honeyed drawl, bright red hair and sharp green eyes left no doubt as to who she was.

'That would be me.' Sandi stuck out her hand. 'You're obviously Kieran's mother. I'm pleased to meet you.'

'Sweetheart, if you're gonna stick with my boy, you'd better get used to our Southern ways. Come here and give me a proper hug.'

'Don't frighten her off.' Kieran appeared and tapped his mother on the shoulder. 'They don't do that here.'

Sandi refused to be pigeonholed. She'd always been stubborn. 'Ignore him. We sometimes make exceptions.' A flash of gratitude lit up the woman's face as she opened her arms, and they exchanged a warm hug.

'She's a good girl. Make sure you keep her.' Maura nodded towards Kieran. It was really hard to suppress a laugh as a fierce blush set his pale freckled skin on fire. He muttered something unintelligible under his breath and stared down at the floor.

'How about some breakfast? You must be starving.' Sandi rattled off the list of what was on offer. 'When you've eaten, you'll have to tell me all about your first impressions of Cornwall.'

'I want to try whatever y'all normally eat. Fix me a plate, and yourself one too, so we can have a good ole chat.' Maura gave Kieran a scathing glance. 'I suppose you'd better cook up some for this hobo as well.'

At a wild guess Sandi would say his mother wasn't impressed by her son's ragged jeans and faded blue shirt. She was always fussy about her own appearance, but Kieran's casual style of dress worked on him, and she couldn't imagine him in a three-piece-suit and tie.

'I'll be happy to. Make yourself at home.' Her cheeks flamed. 'Sorry. I forgot this is your house. I've got used to thinking of it as Kieran's.'

'Don't apologise, honey. I'd come here thinking to make a whole bunch of changes ready to use it for vacations, but now I'm not so sure.'

'Really?' Kieran jumped into the conversation.

'Your daddy hates travelling outside of Tennessee, and … let's just say I can't see me here without him.' She looked sheepish. 'Course, he don't know that yet. I left him dangling when I came here.'

'I thought you wanted to bring your friends here?'

Maura scoffed. 'That was a dumb idea of mine. My old friends would think I was showing off, and the new ones ... let's just say I've seen the light there. I guess I'll give in and buy the lakeside cabin and boat your daddy wants. It'll mean I'll be stuck with spending my weekends sitting on the deck with my head in a book while he's failing to catch fish,' Maura half-heartedly complained.

Kieran hugged his mother. 'You don't know how pleased I am to hear you say all that. I'm sorry, too, that I haven't always been very understanding.'

'You're a good boy. Don't fret.'

Breakfast. She was supposed to be cooking. Sandi went back to the cooker and turned the frying pan on to heat up.

'If you're going to get rid of the house, I'd like to buy it.'

Sandi cracked an egg into the pan and tried to stop herself from jumping up and down with joy. She added another egg to the bubbling oil, and forced herself to concentrate on getting them perfect and not burning the toast.

'Buy it? Sometimes you ain't got the sense God gave a goose.' Maura's warm laughter filled the room. 'Take the place with my blessing. I don't want it, and I'm not gonna pretend I need the money either.'

Sandi shared out the food and picked up two plates to carry over, setting the first down in front of Kieran's mother.

'Has he told you about my big lottery win?'

'A little. You were very fortunate.'

Maura's sad smile spoke volumes. 'For years we lived hand-to-mouth, and I had the crazy idea money would solve all our problems. Boy, was I wrong.'

Sandi pulled out a chair and sat down.

'Gerry and me had barely a cross word in nearly forty years of marriage before I won that money.' She swallowed hard.

'When I left to come here, I told him I wasn't sure I'd be back.' Tears rolled down Maura's face and dripped onto her gaudy yellow silk blouse.

'I'm sure he didn't believe you. I can tell your love for each other is solid and strong. You can make things right again. You need to talk to each other and be honest.' Sandi caught Kieran's eye and hoped he realised she was talking about them too.

'Oh, Mama.' Kieran's voice hitched and he wrapped an arm around his mother's shoulders.

'I was right the first time. You're a good girl.' Maura surprised her with a kiss on the cheek.

'I haven't been much help,' Kieran confessed. 'I've been too wrapped up in my own problems to see what was happening. I couldn't bear to talk about my troubles with y'all because I was afraid I'd fall apart.'

'That's what families are for, Sandi spoke up. 'They're the ones you *can* fall apart with.' She'd certainly done it with her own parents many times, when her marriage failed and looking after Pip alone was hard and lonely.

The phone in the hall jangled and Sandi jumped up to answer it, hoping they'd continue the conversation. When she told the man on the other end that Kieran wasn't available, he ordered her to fetch him. She rushed back to the kitchen. 'Kieran, it's someone called Nick on the phone, and he says he's your manager.'

'Tell him I don't … '

'He said he knows you don't want to talk to him, but he insists you need to listen to something he has to say.'

'Fine,' he grouched, and shoved his chair back out of the way.

Sandi crossed her fingers as he left the room. She'd bet everything she owned that Helen Ross was causing trouble again.

28

Kieran took the stairs two at a time up to his bedroom. He grabbed his laptop from the top of the dresser, perched on the edge of the bed, and quickly logged on. His hands shook as he searched for Helen's name. Nick had told him to read Helen's statement, made alongside her lawyer in Nashville late last night. It was apparently all over the news stations and social media. She'd laid everything on the line and spelled out exactly why she'd lied and accused Kieran of stealing her song. He read it through once, and then several more times to let it fully sink in. Helen's concluding words were that she'd be returning the money she'd received from the out-of-court settlement.

His mother's words about family being more important than money struck home, and he knew what he needed to do. The decision he'd made not to work with

Helen again wasn't going to change, but he couldn't sit by and let her family suffer. He'd tell Nick to arrange a payment to her from his personal bank account. There would be no strings attached, except for making sure that Helen's father couldn't touch the money.

Kieran checked his emails and wasn't sure whether to laugh or cry. The same people who'd turned their backs on him when he was in trouble were all over him now. The messages were all along the same lines — they'd never believed the accusation in the first place, and couldn't wait to work with him again. He deleted every single one without a second thought.

But there were two emails he needed to send. One went to Nick with instructions about what to do on Kieran's behalf. In the second, he thanked Helen for doing the right thing, and wished her well. End of story.

He went over to stand by the window, and a newfound sense of peace swept over him. Through the half-open door he caught drifts of laughter from downstairs, and for the first time in a year a kernel of hope snaked through him.

'Are you all right?' Sandi startled him and he turned to see her hesitating in the doorway. 'We got worried when you didn't return.'

'Come here.' He smiled and beckoned her over. She didn't need asking twice, and when she stepped over to join him, Kieran wrapped his arms around her. 'It's all good. I needed to check a few things on the computer, that's all.' Quietly, he explained about Helen's confession and the actions he'd decided on.

'You're a decent man, and that was the right thing to do.'

'Thanks. I'm not sure I'm quite ready to forgive her, though,' he admitted.

'You will one day.' Sandi's assurance touched him. He'd never had a woman on — or by — his side before, but it felt good. This depth of love was what had held his parents together for decades and would pull them through this latest challenge.

'Have I told you I love you?'

'I don't think you have,' Sandi teased, screwing up her face in a put-on frown. 'I'm sure I'd remember.'

'So?'

'So what?'

'I kind of thought you might say something back. Maybe along the lines of that you love me too?'

'Strictly speaking, you haven't said it to me yet. You merely asked if you'd told me, and I said you hadn't.' Her endearing smile made his heart flip. 'Are you saying now that you actually do love me, and want to know if I feel the same way?'

'You're tying me up in knots,' Kieran protested.

'And you say *I'm* easy to tease.' She gazed up at him, her eyes brimming over with emotion. 'I love you too. Happy now?'

'Yeah. Very.' Kieran grinned. 'I'm glad your mother was right.'

'My mother?'

'She told me weeks ago I had you tied up in knots yourself. It didn't seem like it to me, but I kept on hoping.'

240

'I'll have a word with her later.' Her words were at odds with the brilliant smile lighting up her face. Suddenly a shadow flitted across her eyes, and he knew she'd gone back into worry mode.

'Not yet, sweetheart.'

'What're you talking about?'

'Don't plan too far ahead. We'll sort it out. Okay?'

'I suppose so, but … '

'But nothing.' Kieran's firm reply brought back her smile. 'Right now, we're going downstairs to make another attempt at eating breakfast. I'm starved. While you cook, I'll get my mom up to speed on the whole Helen thing.' He was relieved when she didn't argue. He hadn't had time yet to work out the answers to the thousands of questions Sandi must surely have. They'd do that together. *Together* was the best word ever in his book.

* * *

The stupid smile wouldn't leave her face. Sandi knew it was on there, but couldn't do a thing about it. She wanted to shout from the rooftops that Kieran O'Neill loved her. *Her.* If she thought about it too hard, it didn't make sense.

Then don't think about it too hard, silly.

'Why do I have to wear this itchy shirt?' Pip whined, tugging at the neck.

Sandi didn't want this happy mood to disappear. She took a couple of slow, deep breaths, and patiently explained to her son — yet again — that Kieran and his mother were arriving soon to eat dinner with them.

'I know. But I still hate this shirt.'

If she wasn't careful, Pip would melt down into a full-blown tantrum. Impressing Maura wasn't worth the risk. 'Fine. Go and change into one you like.' Parenting was all about picking the right battles.

'Any one?'

'As long as it's clean.'

Pip beamed and raced off to his

bedroom. Before he came back out, Sandi knew what he'd be wearing — the too-small, washed-a-hundred-times t-shirt with a picture of the solar system's planets that her father had given him for his birthday last year. Instead of fretting, she checked on the roast chicken and hummed to herself as she basted it with a fragrant honey-and-herb glaze. The doorbell rang, but before she could go to answer it, a flash of something blue raced by her.

'Mummy, Mummy, they're here, and they've got flowers and chocolate and …'

'So much for trying to surprise you.' Kieran strolled in brandishing a gorgeous bouquet of peach roses and a huge box of chocolates. 'I don't think we'll get this kid a job as a spy anytime soon.' Maura came in to join them, and Sandi wiped her hands before giving his mother a hug.

She started to apologise for Pip, but Maura brushed away her attempt with her signature warm laugh.

'Young man, I hear you've got a really neat yard, and grow your own flowers and vegetables. Would you show it to me?'

Pip looked puzzled, and Sandi hastened to explain. 'Mrs. O'Neill wants to see our garden.'

'Why didn't she say so?'

'Because she's from America like me, Pip, and we talk funny sometimes,' Kieran said with a chuckle. 'Remember the squash?'

Pip nodded and made a grab for Maura's hand. 'Come on. I'll tell you the proper names for things, and then you'll get it right next time, Mrs. O'Neill.'

Sandi wished she could disappear into a hole in the ground.

'You'll make a good teacher one day.' Maura ruffled Pip's hair. 'And how about you call me Ms. Maura? It's friendlier.'

The two of them disappeared out the back door, leaving Sandi alone with Kieran.

'I've been thinking.'

'Dangerous,' Sandi tried to crack a joke, but couldn't quite bring it off.

'You always jump to the worst conclusions, don't you?' Kieran's wry smile eased some of her anxiety. 'A little bird told me it's Pip's half-term holiday from school next week. My mom's planning to do a few local sightseeing trips, and she's really keen for us to go with her. It'd be a great chance for y'all to get to know each other better. I told her I don't care where else we go, but I've insisted we have one day in Tintagel so Pip and I can indulge our King Arthur fantasies.'

She hated having to be practical. 'I work, remember?'

'Yep, I remember. I know one of your employers will be happy to let you go, and I'm guessing the Copper Kettle can survive for a few days without you, too.' Before she could protest, he laid two fingers on her lips. 'I know you need the money, but will it offend your independence if I assure you I'll take care of that side of things?' He pressed a soft kiss on her forehead. 'I love you and Pip. I want to spoil you both a little. Is that so awful?'

He put it in such a loving way that she couldn't turn him down. Pip would be in seventh heaven. 'I suppose not.'

Kieran's broad grin could've lit up London.

'Let's have dinner first. If you tell Pip now, he'll be too excited to eat.'

'I'm excited too. Do I have to eat?'

Sandi poked him in the ribs. 'You certainly do. I've been slaving over this chicken for hours, so it's the least you can do.'

'Anything you say, sweetheart.'

'Anything?'

He frowned. 'What's your devious brain up to now?'

'That's no way to talk to the woman you're supposed to love.' Sandi's effort to sound hurt obviously failed, because Kieran only smiled. 'I was going to ask you ... '

'Come on. Spit it out.'

She was too nervous to make a smart response. 'Mike and Keri are taking Pip out again tomorrow. I wondered if you'd like to come here to meet them later when they bring Pip back?'

'Sure. I'd be happy to.' Kieran's easy acceptance swept away her concerns as it always did.'

Sandi pushed all her negative thoughts about tomorrow away, and simply enjoyed the moment.

29

Kieran fiddled with the collar of his shirt as he prepared to ring Sandi's doorbell. He'd given in to his mother's insistence that he smarten himself up to meet Mike Tregonning, but had drawn the line at wearing a tie.

It'd been quite a day already. He'd gone to Falmouth with his mother and gone to the bookshop. They'd agreed to let Mr. Rescorla get in touch with his contact in London to authenticate the King Arthur book. Afterwards when they'd returned to the house, she'd asked him to leave her alone while she called his father. From his study Kieran heard her loud sobs all the way as she talked about what a fool she'd made of herself over the lottery money. Slowly, her tears had turned to laughter, and his worries eased. He didn't imagine for a minute that everything was sorted, but he'd sleep easier tonight knowing his parents were back on track again.

'Come in. They'll be here in a minute.' Sandi flung open her front door, grabbed his arm and hauled him into the living room.

'How did you know I was here? Were you watching for me?' he teased.

'Don't be so cocky! I was looking out for Pip.'

He'd recognised the love and gratitude in her eyes when she'd opened the door, but let her get away with the excuse.

'It's just … weird. I'm not sure how Mike will do seeing you. Plus Keri will probably be with him, and I've never met her.' Her voice trailed away, and Kieran finally realised the main reason she'd wanted him here. She was flat-out nervous of meeting Mike's second wife.

'We'll all be fine.' He took hold of her hands and gently stroked the warm skin. 'Mike's happy now, and so are you — I hope. We all want the best for Pip, so it's all good.'

'But she's a doctor, and I … '

'You are a very smart, capable woman, who's brought up a wonderful boy largely on your own.' He kissed her cheek. 'You're also beautiful and a very talented artist.'

'Mummy, we're home.'

'Thanks. You're a wonderful man,' she whispered.

Wonderful. He would take that.

'Kieran, yippee!' Pip burst into the room and raced over to thrust a long narrow box at him. Sandi gave her son a disapproving stare, and he knew he'd have to smooth things out later. Yesterday, he'd suggested that Pip called him by his first name, without okaying it with her — which had been a bad decision. 'Daddy and Keri bought me a new telescope. Isn't it cool?'

'It certainly is. You're a lucky boy.' He glanced over Pip's shoulder, and saw Sandi shaking hands with an elegant blond woman with a friendly smile and pretty grey eyes.

'Kieran, come and meet Mike and Keri.' Sandi's tense voice betrayed her nervousness.

'Sure.' He joined her, and they exchanged pleasantries overlaid with more than a little curiosity on all sides. Mike's building work had kept him in decent shape, and it was obvious where Pip got his unusual combination of startling red hair and warm brown eyes.

'Sandi tells me you're in the music business.'

'Yeah, that's right.' He expanded on his answer, and Keri's eyes widened in surprise.

'When are you returning to Nashville?' Mike's pointed question took him by surprise although he supposed it shouldn't have done.

'I'm not sure. My plans are fluid.' He smiled at Sandi. 'A lot has changed since I came here.'

Mike glanced over at Pip, who was engrossed in opening up the telescope, before turning back to give Kieran a fierce glare. 'Don't you dare to mess my boy around.' He kept his voice low. 'He's obviously fond of you already, and he doesn't need you raising his hopes and not following through.'

Kieran dredged up every ounce of self-control he possessed. 'I don't make promises I can't keep.'

The words hung in the air between them, and a deep flush of embarrassment coloured Mike's pale freckled skin. Redheads could never conceal their emotions, and from personal experience, Kieran knew that could be both a blessing and a curse.

'Mike didn't mean to be rude — did you?' Keri gave her husband a stern stare.

'No. Of course not,' he mumbled. 'I don't want to see him hurt, that's all.' Mike raised his head and met Kieran's gaze straight on. 'I let him down badly enough. I don't want him hurt again. That's all.'

'I love Pip.' Kieran might as well spell it out, whether the other man liked it or not. 'He's a neat kid, and I intend to do right by him. He lowered his voice to make sure Pip didn't hear their conversation. 'I would never try to take your place.'

'Thanks. I appreciate that. I know it's more than I deserve,' Mike grunted. 'We'll be on our way now.'

'Kieran, can you fix this, please? It's broken.' Pip shoved the telescope at him, and a flash of pain creased Mike's face.

'I bet your daddy could do a better job than me. He's good with his hands.'

'Oh. Okay.'

Kieran wasn't seeking the other man's gratitude, but got it anyway in the form of a brief nod. He'd done it for Pip's sake.

'We really must be off now,' Mike said when the telescope was put together properly. He stuck out his hand to Kieran. 'Thanks, mate.'

'No problem.' He hung back while everyone said their goodbyes, and wasn't sorry when he heard the front door close.

'Bathtime and bed, Pip,' Sandi said as soon as she came back in. 'No arguing. Mr. O'Neill will read you one story if you're good.'

'He told me to call … '

'We'll discuss that later.' Her tone of

voice made Pip's face fall into a picture of misery. After she bustled away, Kieran sank down on the sofa and waited.

* * *

Sandi had intended to be firm with both of her men, but failed miserably. Pip persuaded her to let him try out his new telescope 'to make sure it works' and managed to delay bedtime until nearly ten o'clock. Then Kieran, too, twisted her around his little finger with his pathetic apology. Not only had she conceded that Pip could call him by his first name but she'd also agreed to his plans for next week.

Their time spent together, with and without Kieran's mother, would be a real test. They'd find out now how they all got on before things went any further and they considered becoming a family.

This was what she was most afraid of. Although it was often tough and lonely as a single parent, Sandi was used to their life, and it was all Pip had ever known. Kieran's love opened up boundless opportunities for them both, but the question still was whether she had the courage to take such a huge leap of faith.

'You're doing the overthinking thing again, honey,' Kieran remonstrated. He pulled her over to his end of the sofa and wrapped his arms around her. 'I'm trying to live by my new mantra of enjoying every moment and taking each day as it comes.' His green eyes glittered with emotion. 'I've wasted too much time this last year fretting over things I couldn't change.'

'Me too, only I've been doing it for six long years. It's good to learn from the past, but then we need to move on. The future is up in the air, too. I've spent too many sleepless nights worrying about next week, next month and next year. I know I've missed out on a lot, and don't intend to anymore,' she whispered.

The moon shining in through the open window set Kieran's rich coppery hair on fire, and she bathed in the love

30

'Come on, you can make it!'

Sandi seriously considered smacking Kieran. The only problem was, she didn't have the energy. Over the last three days, they'd walked for miles exploring the north coast of Cornwall along with Maura. They'd started with a day in Newquay, where his mother compared the tacky gift shops to those in Gatlinburg, a tourist resort in the Smoky Mountains. Then it'd been the pretty seaside town of Padstow, where they'd eaten at Rick Stein's famous fish and chip shop before taking the short passenger ferry ride over to Rock. She and Maura left the boys to play on the beach while they checked out all the expensive houses and kept their eyes open for anyone famous. Sandi had lost brownie points for failing to produce Prince Harry — Kieran's mother had a huge soft spot for the redheaded prince. Wednesday was devoted to Camelford, which was also on the unofficial Kieran O'Neill King Arthur trail. She'd rolled her eyes at the idea of this sleepy town being the genuine Camelot, but kept her thoughts to herself. Sandi had watched in amused disbelief as Kieran and Pip soaked in every word of the Slaughter Bridge storyteller, who insisted that this was the sight of the final battle between Arthur and Mordred, leading to the demise of the Round Table. After that, Maura declared herself to be 'King Arthured out'. Kieran's mother had stayed in Penarth today, and intended to spend a quiet day around the village and have tea with Sandi's parents.

As soon as they'd arrived in Tintagel this morning, Pip had acted as if he'd been handed the keys to the kingdom.

'We could've done the Great Hall in the town first, and saved the castle for later,' Kieran ventured.

Sandi glanced up at the hundreds of steep steps leading up to the ruined castle. She'd chosen to do this now partly because Pip might otherwise burst with excitement, but also her afternoon plan was to find a quiet teashop where she could rest her weary feet. She intended to send the indefatigable pair off to traipse around a replica of King Arthur's Great Hall without her.

'It'll be worth it for the view. Trust me.'

She met Kieran's gaze and couldn't do anything other than agree.

'We'll get the Land Rover up from the visitors' centre afterwards. Promise.'

So far, they'd passed the togetherness test with flying colours. Pip was blossoming in ways she could only have imagined, and Kieran's bottomless patience with her son made Sandi fall more in love with him every minute. No question was too trivial, and he gave equal weight to both explaining to Pip why there were rainbows, and answering his persistent questions about every single one of King Arthur's knights — about whom Kieran had an encyclopaedic knowledge.

'What are you staring at?' he broke through her wandering thoughts.

You. You're the best man on earth, and I don't know how I got so lucky.

'Hey, I'm the lucky one.'

His deep understanding of her didn't faze Sandi now.

Kieran grabbed her hand. 'Only about another eighty steps to go.'

'Isn't it dangerous?'

'Only if we're not careful; and Pip knows the rules, don't you?'

'Yes, Kieran. I must always hold yours or Mummy's hand. *Don't run, and don't go any closer to the edge of the cliff than you do,*' Pip carefully recited every word.

'See. We're good.' Kieran's smile was infectious, and she couldn't help grinning right back at him. 'I won't talk any more, then you won't have to answer me. Let's just do this.'

★ ★ ★

Kieran's plan had to work. He'd plotted and schemed for the last few days. He

260

had talked it over with both of their mothers, and come to the conclusion this was the perfect spot.

He winked at Pip, and the little boy beamed as he recognised his cue.

'Mummy, I want to see where that door goes.' He pointed to a crumbling stone archway.

Sandi frowned. 'Well, I … '

'Sure. Come on,' Kieran agreed.

'Is *your* name Mummy now?'

He ignored the sarcastic comeback and took hold of both their hands. 'Let's check it out.' Luckily, there was no one else around at the moment, because he didn't want an audience. Once they made their way over the uneven stones and stepped through the arch, a stunning view opened up in front of them. He'd checked it out online, but that was nothing compared to seeing it in real life. The rugged cliffs dropped away dramatically to the sea where the water reflected today's Mediterranean blue sky.

'Wow.' Sandi exhaled a happy sigh.

Just go for it.

'Sandi,' he croaked and dropped to the ground. Possibly not his smartest idea, because he caught his knee on a rock and hastily bit back a word Pip didn't need to hear.

'Let's take a picture.' Sandi kept on staring out at the sea until he was afraid his leg would seize up.

'Mummy!' Pip tugged on her hand, jumping up and down. 'Kieran wants to marry us and be a family. I told him yes.'

'You what?' Sandi shrieked, and finally turned around and paid attention to Kieran. 'What on earth are you … ' Her face flamed. 'Oh.' She flung her hands up to cover her face and peeked out between her fingers.

'Don't you move an inch, Pip,' Kieran ordered. Her son falling off the cliff in the middle of things wasn't going to convince Sandi he was good stepfather material. Prising open the jewellery box he'd stuffed into his jeans pocket, his hands shook as he struggled to get the ring out. 'This might be unorthodox, but

I asked Pip for your hand in marriage instead of your father because I reckoned he has a higher stake.'

'Dare I ask how my wonderful son replied?' Sandi's voice wavered and she clearly couldn't believe this was happening.

He laughed. 'Pip asked why I didn't want the rest of you, and what I was going to do with just your hand.'

'Oh, Pip.' She reached out and ruffled his hair.

'I explained it was an old saying and not to be taken literally.' Kieran fixed her with his gaze, wanting to push everything else away for a few precious seconds. 'I assured him I most definitely do want every single inch of you.'

'Put the ring on, Mummy, I helped to choose it. So did Granny and Mommy Maura.'

'They all know?' she whispered.

'Yeah. I figured this was a family affair. None of us lives in a vacuum, so why get engaged in one?'

'Engaged? Is that what we are?'

'If you ever say yes, we will be.' Kieran groaned and shifted awkwardly on the rough ground. 'Although, if you take much longer to decide, you'll have to call out the emergency services to haul me back up to standing.'

She peered into the box at the stunning sapphire-and-diamond ring. 'It's very pretty.' Sandi held out her hand, and the smile she gave him shot straight to Kieran's heart. 'I don't want to be responsible for injuring you, so I'll say yes. But I ... '

'Don't say another word. We can sort out the details later. Enjoy the moment. Remember?' He wriggled the ring on over her finger and struggled to his feet. 'Come here, Pip.' Kieran pulled them both into his arms. 'You've both made me the happiest man in the world.'

Life was good.

* * *

'No. I'm sorry, but I can't take any of the money for Pip.' Sandi shook her head. A few minutes earlier, Kieran had received a phone call from the bookshop in Falmouth while they were having tea, and he'd stunned her for the second time that day. He'd suspected that the book Pip found in Peter Trudgeon's house could be valuable, but hadn't said anything to her until it could be proved one way or the other. An expert in London had confirmed it was a genuine, rare first edition, and worth upwards of two million pounds.

'Honey. It's only right for my family to share this with him. I might never have discovered it on my own. It's fair.' He squeezed her hand. 'Put it in a trust fund for him that he can't touch until he's grown up. You've worried about money for so long, so you must know what this would mean for him. Look at me, sweetheart,' he pleaded. 'I didn't mean to offend you.'

'You didn't. I'm simply overwhelmed.' Sandi hesitated and glanced over at Pip, who was stuffing a cream doughnut into his mouth and trying to read at the same time. The new book Kieran had bought him in one of the gift shops on his favourite knight, Sir Lancelot, was obviously riveting.

'Out with it.'

'Okay. I suppose it's a mad thing to say, but … do you actually *need* the money?'

Kieran looked mystified. 'Well, no. I'm not bragging, but I'm fine; and so are my folks these days.'

'Pip doesn't need it either. I'd prefer him to make his own way in life the same as we've both had to. If your mother is agreeable, how about donating the book to the British Museum instead of selling it to one rich person who'll keep it hidden away in their private collection?' She smiled. 'That way, you, Pip, and all the other King Arthur lovers can enjoy it on display. I have the feeling your great-uncle would approve.'

'You are one special lady.' He kissed her. 'It's a brilliant solution, and I'm sure Mom will think so too. She'll certainly say they don't need any more money.' Kieran played with her hair. She'd left it loose again today around her shoulders because he preferred it that way. 'Have you given any more thought to Pip's suggestion for our wedding venue?'

She'd been persuaded to join Kieran and Pip on their visit to 'King Arthur's Great Halls', and as soon as her son set foot inside the door, his eyes went the size of giant saucers. The Great Hall, with its Arthurian-themed stained glass windows, colourful banners, massive round wooden table with all the knight's names engraved around the edge, and elaborate stone throne, was impressive. When the guide mentioned that the building was licensed for weddings, Pip's excitement bubbled over and he'd pleaded with them to get married there.

Sandi couldn't find it in her heart to say no. If wearing a medieval dress and gnawing on a turkey leg would make her two favourite men happy, then that was what she'd do.

'I love you, and Pip will never forget this.' Kieran planted a soft kiss on her mouth.

'But I didn't ... '

'You don't need to, honey. You love us both too much to refuse.' He beamed. 'Do you know one thing we need when we redecorate the kitchen at *Gwel an Mor?* A round table.'

'Oh, we definitely do.' Sandi kissed him, not caring who was watching. Loyal. Chivalrous. Handsome. Brave and loving. Kieran would never let her down.

'Can you teach me how to fight with a sword?' Pip looked up from his book.

She watched Kieran suppress a smile and take Pip's question seriously, as he always did. There followed an intent discussion on Kieran's lack of prowess with a sword, and where they could both go to learn when Pip was a little older. A wave of love swept over Sandi, and any lingering doubts disappeared. This wonderful unexpected love had come into their lives, and nothing would ever be the same again. And for that, she couldn't be more grateful.

We do hope that you have enjoyed reading this large print book.

Did you know that all of our titles are available for purchase?

We publish a wide range of high quality large print books including:
Romances, Mysteries, Classics
General Fiction
Non Fiction and Westerns

Special interest titles available in large print are:
The Little Oxford Dictionary
Music Book, Song Book
Hymn Book, Service Book

Also available from us courtesy of Oxford University Press:
Young Readers' Dictionary
(large print edition)
Young Readers' Thesaurus
(large print edition)

For further information or a free brochure, please contact us at:
Ulverscroft Large Print Books Ltd.,
The Green, Bradgate Road, Anstey,
Leicester, LE7 7FU, England.
Tel: (00 44) 0116 236 4325
Fax: (00 44) 0116 234 0205

LOVE IN A MIST

Margaret Mounsdon

Minnie Hyde — flame-haired beauty and acclaimed actress of her day — leaves a legacy of confusion when she dies without a will. Penny Graham, a single parent running a pet-grooming parlour in a disused theatre on the land, is soon threatened with eviction by Minnie's grandson, Roger Oakes. That is, until long-lost Australian granddaughter Sarah Deeds also lays claim to the estate. Amidst the confusion, Penny must deal with her growing feelings for a man who would make her homeless . . .

THE DANCE OF LOVE

Jean Robinson

Starting a new phase in her life after the death of her chronically ill mother, Carrie decides to go on a cruise to Alaska. All the other passengers seem to be in couples, though, and she immediately feels left out. Then she meets fellow lone passenger Tom, who becomes a firm friend — until the handsome and elusive Greg steals her heart. Should Carrie take a chance on him, or accept the security offered by Tom? And what will happen when the cruise comes to an end?

SHEARWATER COVE

Sheila Spencer-Smith

When her cousin asks for help with running his holiday business in the Isles of Scilly, Lucy Cameron is happy to oblige. On the ferry there, she meets Matt Henderson, an attractive local marine biologist — but is appalled by his work. Soon the sea air, soft sands, and friendly locals make Lucy feel welcome; and as she gets to know Matt, she's tempted to see him in a better light. Lucy's stay at Polwhenna is temporary, though — and as the time to go home creeps closer, she is increasingly torn . . .

ROSES FOR ROBINA

Eileen Knowles

Brett had been the love of Robna's life — until he disappeared without a word. But now he's back in Little Prestbury, to attend his brother's funeral and take on the running of the family estate. And Robbie has to work with him . . . How will her boyfriend Richard react — and how will she cope? Despite telling anyone who'll listen — herself included — that she's over Brett, Robina just can't seem to stop thinking about him . . .

A LOVE DENIED

Louise Armstrong

1815: Felix, Earl of Chando, sets out to engage a suitable companion for his much-loved mother. He finds her in Miss Phoebe Allen, whose charm and good nature win him over. Once at Elwood, Phoebe also takes on the muddled household accounts, and advises Felix on how he can save the ailing estate. Felix finds himself falling in love with her — but he is determined never to marry, as he fears there is bad blood in his family. Will Phoebe change his mind?